The Man Who Swam with Beavers

The Man
Who Swam
with Beavers

STORIES

NANCY LORD

Coffee House Press

2001

COFFEE HOUSE PRESS is an independent nonprofit literary publisher supported in part by a grant provided by the Minnesota State Arts Board, through an appropriation by the Minnesota State Legislature, and in part by a grant from the National Endowment for the Arts. Support has also been provided by Athwin Foundation; the Bush Foundation; Elmer L. & Eleanor J. Andersen Foundation; Honeywell Foundation; James R. Thorpe Foundation; Lila Wallace-Reader's Digest Fund; McKnight Foundation; Patrick and Aimee Butler Family Foundation; Pentair, Inc.; The St. Paul Companies Foundation, Inc.; the law firm of Schwegman, Lundberg, Woessner & Kluth, P.A.; Star Tribune Foundation; the Target Foundation; West Group; and many individual donors. To you and our many readers across the country, we send our thanks for your continuing support.

COFFEE HOUSE PRESS books are available to the trade through our primary distributor, Consortium Book Sales & Distribution, cbsd.com or (800) 283-3572 For personal orders, catalogs, or other information, write to info@coffeehousepress.org.

LIBRARY OF CONGRESS CIP INFORMATION
Lord, Nancy.
The man who swam with beavers : stories / Nancy Lord.
p. cm.
ISBN 1-56689-110-8 (alk. paper)
1. Alaska—Social life and customs—Fiction.   I. Title.
PS3562.O727 M3 2001
813'.54—DC21
00-065895

PRINTED IN THE UNITED STATES OF AMERICA

10 9 8 7 6 5 4 3 2

The main motifs of the myths are the same,
and they have always been the same.

—JOSEPH CAMPBELL

Contents

Acknowledgments

THIS WORK OF FICTION was largely inspired by the titles and themes of stories belonging to Native Americans, particularly Alaska's Athabaskans. Some of the source stories classify as creation myths or stories from the time when people and animals talked together, others as history, and yet others as fictional tales; in general, they tend to illustrate moral lessons. I'm grateful for their wisdom.

The title "The Attainable Border of the Birds" comes from a Chukchi story in Howard Norman's *Northern Tales: Traditional Stories of Eskimo and Indian Peoples* (Pantheon, 1994).

"The Woman Who Would Marry a Bear" found its inspiration in many Northwest coast versions of "The Woman Who Married a Bear." Two of these narratives, by Tom Peters and Frank Dick, Sr., are included in *Haa Shuka, Our Ancestors: Tlingit Oral Narratives*, edited by Nora Marks Dauenhauer and Richard Dauenhauer (University of Washington Press, 1987).

The original "The Man Who Went Through Everything" is a story collected in several partial versions in *Tales from the Dena: Indian Stories from the Tanana, Koyukuk, and Yukon Rivers*, edited by Frederica de Laguna (University of Washington Press, 1995). The original is also known as the Saga of the Traveler, a widely told and very old story cycle of many episodes or incidents, in which a man (sometimes characterized as a bungler, sometimes as a culture hero or shaman) makes a long and transforming journey down a river.

"Wolverine Grudge" was inspired by the Woodland Cree story, "The Wolverine Grudge," collected in Howard Norman's *Northern Tales*, referenced above.

"What Was Washing Around out There" incorporates, in a very abbreviated form, two stories found in *Tales from the Dena*, referenced above. The first, "The Girl Who Went to the Sky," was told by John

Silas in Nenana in 1935, and the second, "Crow and a Whale Story," was told by John Dayton in Koyukuk Station in the same year.

"Behold" was influenced in part by "Edge of the Earth and the Hole in the Sky" in Robert Mayokok's *Eskimo Stories* (self-published).

The original "The Baby Who, According to His Aunt, Resembled His Uncle" is found in *Bakk'aatugh Ts'uhuhiy: Stories We Live By*, traditional Koyukon Athabaskan stories told by Catherine Attla (Alaska Native Language Center, 1989). The original concerned Crow outwitting Brown Bear.

"White Bird" makes use of the powerful raven motif of various Northwest cultures and references a bit of history from early contact with the sailing ships of Russian and English explorers.

"Afterlife" makes use of various stories concerning the need to show proper respect to animals. One example can be found in *K'tl'egh'i Sukdu: A Dena'ina Legacy*, the collected writings of Peter Kalifornsky (Alaska Native Language Center, 1991). That story, "Beliefs in Things a Person Can See and in Things a Person Cannot See," illustrates traditional Dena'ina Athabaskan beliefs about the proper treatment of animals.

"Candace Counts Coup" was inspired by the White River Sioux story, "Brave Woman Counts Coup," in *American Indian Myths and Legends*, selected and edited by Richard Erodes and Alfonso Ortiz (Pantheon, 1984).

"The Girl Who Dreamed Only Geese" comes from the title of a children's book by Howard Norman (*The Girl Who Dreamed Only Geese, & Other Tales of the Far North*, Harcourt Brace, 1997). The original story of that name was told to Norman by Billy Nuuq, of Churchill, Manitoba.

The original "Why Owls Die with Wings Outspread" is a Swampy Cree story collected in Howard Norman's *Northern Tales*, referenced above.

"The Man Who Swam with Beavers" was inspired by "First Beaver Story" in *Tanaina Tales from Alaska*, by Bill Vaudrin (University of Oklahoma Press, 1981).

The original "Remaking the World" is a Brule Sioux story collected in *American Indian Myths and Legends*, referenced above.

The remaining stories reference "myths" and legends that surround historical figures—Jack London, Walt Disney, and Anton Chekhov.

The Mythology of North America: Introduction to Classic Native American Gods, Heroes & Tricksters by John Bierhorst (William Morrow and Company, 1985) provided me with a very helpful overview of the traditional stories of Native Americans and a context within which to try to understand the purpose and development of myth, ancient and modern.

Some of these stories first appeared in the following journals: "The Woman Who Would Marry a Bear" in *Kinesis*, "The Man Who Swam with Beavers" in *International Quarterly*, "White Bird" in *The Great River Review*, "Recall of the Wild" as "Call of the What?" in *The North American Review*, "The Attainable Border of the Birds" in *America West*, and "The Census Taker" in *Prairie Schooner*.

I wish to thank the Ucross Foundation for support of this project.

The Man Who Swam with Beavers

The Attainable Border of the Birds

IN HIS RETIREMENT, John reengaged a childhood passion for birds. He and his wife filled their spacious New Hampshire yard with feeders and birdhouses, started life lists, and joined both their local and state Audubon groups. They braved winter snows to participate in the Christmas bird counts, and they took a weekly watch along the river, every Thursday from nine to eleven, to document eagle sightings. They called in to the bird hotline (655-PEEP) to report the first blue herons of spring and a late cardinal. Once a year, they traveled on organized trips to major birding sites that included the Pribolof Islands in Alaska, the rain forest of Costa Rica, the Everglades, and the moors of England, where the melting cry of a nightingale called up a passage of deeply recessed Milton (*O nightingale, that on yon blooming spray/Warbl'st at eve, when all the woods are still . . .*) and made John weep.

John was, however, not so interested in compiling a life list as he was in simply enjoying birds. So many of the other birders, he'd found, only wanted to collect bird sightings the way they might collect stamps or pairs of shoes or fortunes, taking them into possession with a check mark and then going after more. He found it strange, and annoying, the way they would give one glance to an accidental short-tailed albatross off the coast of Alaska and then retire for coffee until their leader called them for the next sighting, while he and Ruth remained outside, surrounded at the ship's rail by that albatross and a swarm of other magnificent seabirds that coasted on enormous scythe-shaped wings and dipped into the tops of foamy waves. On that same trip, he never tired of watching the tufted and horned puffins dive like little penguins out of the ship's path, even after he'd seen hundreds of pairs. At home he was the same way, delighted with each chickadee at the feeder, with every coo of a mourning dove, with any chance to bend back branches and look into the gaping mouths of naked baby sparrows in a tightly woven nest in which he might, moreover, recognize strands of wool he and Ruth had put out for just that purpose. It was not numbers he was after but finding patterns and learning the connections: with weather, with food, between predator and prey. He liked meeting and remeeting individual birds: a one-legged starling, a woodpecker that drummed on the same hollow tree every April morning at six, the pair of loons that lost one chick but raised the other.

During these bird years, John loved life as he had not for a very long time—since, in fact, he'd been a child. His fondest boyhood memories, which flooded back to him once he began to look at birds again, involved feasting on mulberries from within a tree-swinging, fruit-gobbling, crayon-colored flock of cedar waxwings and hanging around a swamp to watch herons stalk and spear frogs. He often found himself wondering why he'd ever become an orthopedic surgeon, though he supposed the answer was that he'd lacked imagination. When he'd reached the age of seriousness, he'd thought only of supporting a wife and family, and somehow he'd decided that medicine would be a sure way to do that. He hadn't liked the hours of obstetrics or the grimness of oncology, but setting bones had seemed to him a kind of mechanical work he could be good at.

He *was* good, practicing his craft day after day for forty years. When he came home from his office or the hospital, he read medical magazines, and when he and Ruth went away somewhere, it was always to medical meetings.

Ruth, though, besides raising the children and doing everything at home and volunteering at the hospital, had always kept bird feeders in the yard, and every other year, on the schedule she directed, he dutifully climbed up on a ladder and cleaned out her swallow nesting boxes. Once he splinted the broken leg of one of the kids' found nestlings, but the poor thing died anyway and caused a level of household bereavement that made him want to never again come to the aid of anything less than mammalian.

But that was then, before the day he'd stopped working and the great choking fog of pointlessness had closed around him. After that, he had sat at home, suddenly aware that he was not in fact going to take up cooking or golf or cribbage playing. He wasn't, in fact, interested or skilled in any of those things or anything else he could think of, and the medical magazines that lay on the carpet beside him, which he'd thought he was so eager to catch up on, became clearly, undeniably, and utterly trivial, of less use to him than hair rollers. He had sat at home, and though he was only sixty-five years old and in good health, he thought he must be ready to die.

Ruth, that same day, had handed him a coat and said, "We're going for a walk," and he'd followed her out of the house and away to the shore of a freshly frozen lake, where they'd watched a huge bird float down out of the sky, land its plump breast on the black ice, and slide for a hundred feet before coming to a stop. A little sucking sound caught at the back of Ruth's throat. "It thought it was open water," Ruth said to him. "Now it won't be able to take flight again."

He hadn't a clue what she was talking about. It was a bird; why couldn't it just flap its wings and take off? That's when she told him about loons, and their solid, heavy bones, which let them operate so easily underwater; the corollary was that they couldn't launch themselves into the air except by running across the surface of water, peddling with their feet as they furiously flapped their wings. He'd been astounded that she knew such a thing. The loon sat on the middle of the lake, perfectly still, its breast pressed to the ice and its legs folded behind it, and there was no open water anywhere.

In the end, between Ruth's thinking and his instruction following, they'd borrowed a plastic boat that he'd pushed onto the ice, ready to take refuge in it the second he broke through. The ice, however, held until he reached the loon, which only stared at him with unflinching eyes before he dropped a blanket over it and lifted it into the boat in his leather-gloved retired surgeon's hands. He'd walked the boat back to shore while Ruth pulled a rope attached to the bow, and then they had a loon that they drove on a two-hour journey to the open Atlantic Ocean. Dignified, it took its car ride with its head up, sighting across its dagger of a bill. Even in plain brown, out of its breeding plumage of black-and-white dots and dashes and squares, it had been a fabulous feathered animal. As they watched it run across the seawater and take to the air, John had felt a wave of satisfaction akin to having completed a difficult and successful operation, only better.

John had thought they'd go on like this for years, he and Ruth together, filling their bird feeders, taking their trips, watching birds. He knew, of course, that they'd slow down, that he was destined eventually for at least one artificial hip, and that Ruth's eyesight wasn't what it once had been. But she stuck to her estrogen replacement regimen and her calcium pills, and he made sure they both got daily weight-bearing exercise. They were planning a trip to Antarctica to look for king and chin-strap penguins when Ruth had a stroke and died without regaining consciousness.

John was, of course, devastated. He felt his wife's absence like a gaping hole in his side, a hole that seemed to enlarge the farther it went into him, so that his center was very nearly a great echoing hollow. He did not know how to live without her, and on the most practical level he hadn't the slightest idea how to care for himself. He knew, with embarrassment, that he was of that last generation of men served slavishly by women, but the fact remained that he had never in his life cooked a meal, done a load of laundry, or sat at the kitchen table or anywhere else to pay bills. He did not know where his clothes went when Ruth took them to the cleaners or what determined what went to the cleaners and what was washed at home. Grocery stores scared the hell out of him.

On top of all those things that he'd never learned, he began to suffer from memory loss of the short-term kind. He would not remember, five minutes later, what someone had said to him, or he would forget, once he stood up to get something, what it was he meant to get. He had, in fact, given up most dri-ving before Ruth's stroke; when he did drive, he depended upon her for complete, turn-by-turn directions. With her gone, he was afraid to go out or even answer the phone, and after he blew up the microwave oven with a foil-wrapped dish brought by a woman he knew he was supposed to know but couldn't for the life of him put a name or association to, it became apparent to everyone that things would have to change.

That was how John had come to his new home in a retirement center. He supposed that the place was very nice, for what it was. He had his own apartment, with a living room, bedroom, closet, bath, and a small kitchen he didn't need because he took all his meals in the dining room, where young people called him by his first name and were very prompt about bringing him anything on the day's menu. His daughter had arranged everything for him and was good about calling and being cheerful, and he knew he should be grateful.

Still.

John sat in his living room, in the armchair he'd pushed around to face the sliding glass door, and looked out across his miniature porch with its two plastic chairs to the paved parking lot and, in the distance, to a line of scraggly pines. The glass door provided the only natural light for the narrow room, into which no actual direct sunlight made its way. He had told his daughter, in a manner he hoped did not sound too much like complaining, "there's no outdoors to this place." Some witless architect had designed the round building, which had been dropped in the thick of western Massachusetts woods, to look inward—to the dining room, beauty parlor, gift shop, activity room, exercise spa, and fake fireplace in the middle; the builders had suspended deep overhangs over all the exterior doors and windows, and then had surrounded the whole complex with a paved parking lot and circular drive. There was no grass, no garden, not so much as a goddamned flowerbox in sight. There was no place to walk or anywhere to go, unless you were to walk to your car and drive away, which was not an option for John.

He knew it was spring, because he had a calendar. And because, when the sun got around to his side of the building in the afternoon, he could open his sliding glass door and feel warm air radiating off the parking lot, along with the smell of its asphalt. Otherwise, he wouldn't have known. Aside from the distant treetops and occasional people coming and going from their cars, there was no living thing in sight of his porch. He could hear no children calling, no dogs barking, no lawn mowers mowing. No birds singing. There were no birds. Once, he saw a hawk circling in the sky, but otherwise the pavement formed a dead zone around the silent, soundproofed building.

Now he knew what a patient in an isolation ward felt like. Or someone in prison. Or someone dead—though he was sure anyone's conception of heaven had to include singing birds.

He was back to where he'd been the day he'd retired, only he was without Ruth and all of the life that had been possible for him because of Ruth, and he knew, as he seemed not to have known before, what he was without. He recalled perfectly well the details of days when Ruth and he had wandered in woods and fields after yellow-bellied sapsuckers and indigo buntings and had found, besides, the season's first mayflowers, a fox with a hugely bushy red tail, their own laughing friendship.

Day after day, John sat in his chair and waited for breakfast, lunch, dinner, whatever the next meal was. When the time came he went to the dining room and sat with people he didn't know or remember. He listened to them talk about investments, heart conditions, and other people whom he also didn't know. He listened to them list foreign trips they'd made but about which they never seemed to remember anything more than the names of cities and, maybe, hotels, and he wondered, before he forgot all about it himself, why they went to such places if it was only to say they'd gone.

The retirement center offered various activities, but John did not care to sign up for the group trips, which were generally to shopping malls, or to participate in the group singalongs, which were jolly and juvenile, or to attend the crafts sessions, which were also juvenile, consisting mainly of potholder weaving. Neither did he want to play cards, ride a bicycle that didn't go anywhere, or sit in a big vibrating bathtub with strangers. He ate and he napped and he waited for the next meal or to sleep, and sometimes he watched a nature program on the television or read a magazine, but when he turned off the television or put down the magazine, whatever he'd found there ran right out of his mind, like water through a leaky bucket. He thought then of the Inuit people, who, when their elders weren't good for anything anymore, would move camp and leave them behind. The old people, because they knew that was the way to best assure the clan's survival, didn't seem to object. He imagined how they sat out there on the tundra, surrounded by lapland longspurs and snowy owls, and sang their sacred songs to themselves until they died of hunger or exposure and were scavenged by wolves. His highly evolved people were, as far as he was concerned, both less practical and less compassionate.

The weather, what he could tell of it, was weird that spring—hot too soon and then cold and rainy. One day in April the temperature plummeted and the wind came up, and snow began to fall in big gluey gobs. John sat behind his sliding door and watched it come down in swirls, thicker and thicker. Within minutes it covered the pavement outside and the cars in the lot and began to drift up over his little porch.

A bird—a robin—skipped past as though flung by the wind, and then another, and then the whole arena outside his door, in all the thickening, slanting whiteness, became filled with flocks of robins, all leaping and dashing and massing together, all moving past in the same direction, driven by the wind and snow. Hundreds. After a while, maybe thousands.

John sat riveted at his door, watching. Just robins. Just common redbreasted American robins, those same everyday birds he'd seen all his life, tilting their heads on one lawn or another and flying in and out of trees. He noticed now, for perhaps the first time, what gorgeous birds they truly were. Against the snow, their breasts glowed like orange lanterns, their backs layered into soft shades of slate. When they flew, their wing feathers fanned in a way that reminded him of oriental paintings, and their heads stretched with a kind of elegance. They hopped, they flocked, they landed by the dozens in the snow outside his door, they launched again one by one and in groups, in silence. They did not look particularly bewildered by the weather; they looked plump, sturdy, strong. From time to time one or several blew onto his little porch and sheltered there for a minute, looking out at the storm or in at—he didn't know which—either their reflections in the glass or him, in his chair, in his room. He watched the way the wind parted their feathers, but mostly he noticed their eyes—how liquid they were, how dark with glistening and nervy determination.

It was after that when he began to notice that other people, like birds, had distinguishing characteristics he could learn. He looked at their noses as he looked at beaks, at their dresses and ties and shoes as he'd once learned to study wing linings and eye stripes. Bill, one of the men in the dining room, had a nose like a crossbill, overhanging his lip, and the rosy male crossbill's coloring. This was something John could remember—bill and Bill, and, when he learned Bill had been a lawyer, *bill*, as in the outrageous fees that lawyers collected. He noticed Walt, who wore bow ties and white shirts as surely as meadowlarks wore black Vs against yellow breasts, and began to sit with him at meals. A woman named Margaret chattered like a magpie, and he began calling her Maggie, which made her blush like a schoolgirl. He found out, moreover, that some of these people, as different from one another as hawks and warblers and wood ducks, were really quite interesting: Walt had worked for the F.B.I. and still advised on polygraph tests, and one of the ladies, wrenlike in her modesty, had written a series of political biographies. He couldn't always or even usually remember what his new friends told him, but neither could they, and so they all had a lot of fun talking again and reminding one another of different things.

Pretty soon John found himself going along on one of the shopping mall trips. He bought bird feeders and houses, and with a little help from his friends, put these up on his porch and on the light poles in the parking lot and on posts and trees around the circular drive. It didn't take long for the birds to find their way in from the trees; chickadees and jays and purple finches gathered for sunflower seeds, and bluebirds and swallows soared overhead, plucking mosquitoes from the sky. Other people in the retirement center put up their own feeders on their own little porches and came to John to ask his advice on what binoculars to buy. The next thing John knew, he was in charge of the list of bird sightings posted in the dining room, the list that everyone gathered around each day, coming and going for meals. Some of the people who still drove began taking carloads to Audubon meetings and to look for eagles at a nearby reservoir and then for longer birding walks whenever anyone wanted to go, and pretty soon the center itself began to schedule trips to bird sanctuaries and beaver ponds. The crafts program bought handsaws and hammers, and teams of birdhouse builders went at it day and evening, cutting and nailing and painting houses they sold at craft fairs; the considerable money they earned went to a conservation group for the purchase of wetlands habitat. Out in the parking lot, John tied red ribbons around the light poles and hung hummingbird feeders. Other people built raised flower beds, as parking space dividers.

Today, when John isn't out birding, or updating the bird list on the computer, or designing and building bird feeders, or working on the new nature trail that winds through the woods on the east side of the drive, or volunteering at a nearby raptor center, where he helps the veterinarian repair broken wings, you may find him on his little porch, among the seed and suet and sweetwater eaters who gather there. If you're lucky, he may slide his door all the way open, and the ruby-throated hummingbirds will follow him inside to the vases and pots of flowers that all the ladies in the retirement home keep giving him. There, with hummingbirds buzzing around like bees, you may join John in the center of his quite wonderful life.

Recall of the Wild

BUCK, BUCKY, BUCKAROO did not read the newspapers, and so he didn't know about the government's plans for shooting wolves. The wolves ate caribou, but people ate caribou, too, and when there were more people who wanted caribou than there were caribou to be taken, it was plain to the government that the wolves would have to take fewer. The way for wolves to take fewer caribou was for them to *be* fewer—that is, wolves would have to be killed.

On a snowless gray morning at the start of winter, Buck stood on the sidewalk outside a sky-filling government building in Anchorage. All around him people in parkas and knit hats waved signs at passing motorists. The signs said *Stop the Wolf Kill, Control Hunters Not Wolves,* and *Boycott Alaska's Tourism.* Someone walked by with a steaming cup of hot coffee and a cinnamon roll, and Buck pulled ever so gently on his leash, just testing.

The opposite end of his leash was tied to his person's waist and didn't yield, and so Buck went back to watching traffic, the hypnotizing rotations of tires on the wet pavement, the spray of water squeezed behind the rubber with a moist purr. He stood four-footed on the sidewalk, his head lower than his shoulders, his gray eyes fixed, and watched each car roll past. Something in the dull dark back of his brain was ready, alert to the smaller compact, the car that slowed to a stagger at the corner, another with squishy, underinflated tires. He could pick these out, knew there was something about them that interested him. Saliva filled the space under his tongue and dripped between his teeth.

A woman and boy stopped to pet him, and he wondered, as he always did, what sort of people allowed their children to approach strange animals. The boy was no higher than his own large head, and Buck could, if he wished, crush the child's skull rather easily with the power of his jaws, or rip his throat, or tear apart his smooth fearless face. Instead, he turned away, aloof, and allowed the two pairs of hands to fondle the silver-tipped fur along his back, the thick ruff at his neck. His person explained, as she had a million times before, that he was a wolf hybrid, half wolf. His parentage was actually more complicated than that, involving husky, shepherd, and a village dog or two along the way, but he was certainly part wolf, and looked like one, with his long legs and high back, his narrow muzzle, his indisputably intelligent eyes.

"Bucky-boo," his person murmured. "My buckaroo boy." She scratched the top of his head, right where he liked it, and he swept his bushy tail back and forth.

The people waved their signs and chanted. *Stop the slaughter. Stop the slaughter. Stop the slaughter.* Shoppers walked between them, amused, or concerned, or looking away. Cars beeped their horns. An older Native woman wearing a fur *parky* stepped slowly through the crowd, her bare hands locked on the handles of two shopping bags that plunged to one side and the other, nearly touching the ground, with each mincing step. A bearded man in a beaver hat stopped to argue with the demonstrators, then walked away, shaking his head. "Wolves have rights, too!" someone shouted after him.

Buck sat down close to the curb, his tail tucked safely

against his body. His mouth fell open into a nervous, steamy panting; he wasn't accustomed to being in the center of so much activity. At home, in the fenced yard of his person's small wood-sided house, he knew perfectly the length of his chain, every magpie he guarded his dish against, the smells that were his own. The cars went faster here, in thicker, noisier groupings, and trackless gray pavement stretched as far as he could see. He leaned toward a narrow strip of grass that ran between the walk and the street, and sniffed, but the grass, despite its denseness, was icy dead, odorless. He would have leaned all the way, nose to ground, except for the tug of his leash, his umbilical connection.

He stayed leaning, the pull tight and comforting against his neck, and watched a squat brown dachshund round the corner and make its leashed way along the far sidewalk. Buck found something vaguely appealing about the other dog, though he wasn't sure if what he wanted from it had to do with musky smells and a fixing operation he only vaguely remembered having, or with his one true appetite. He imagined closing his jaws on the back of that fatty neck, a snap, a couple of fast chomps, hot raw meat in his stomach, better than all the grease from all the roasting pans he'd ever licked.

The people talked among themselves and held their stick signs high, pitching and dipping them as though they would fly them like kites into wind. Buck squinted his eyes and wished for a Frisbee flung hard down the length of a far field, for the hard bite of plastic in his teeth. The people chanted again, and then they laid their heads back, exposing smooth, whitest necks, and they howled. His person crouched beside him, her lips extended into a snouty pig-faced pucker only a whisker length from his face. She howled, and the others howled, high and low and rumbly, long and righteous. They didn't sound like wolves, or dogs very much, or coyotes, but still there was something in the dissonance of their song that roused an old ambition in Buck. He whimpered and licked his lips.

"C'mon, Bucky-baby," she said. "Do your thing. Help us out here."

He heard the howls all edging into and overlapping one another, yippy and mournful and crooning, and he put his own head back and let loose one more sad and separate cry.

The bull moose was gigantic and magnificent, with a powerful chest and antlers that blocked the light. For days Buck had been following it through deep snow, nipping and giving chase, never allowing it a moment's rest. It was his largest prey yet, and he was determined to bring it down, to make the kill, to feast to his heart's content. He drooled in his anticipation, as he crouched and waited—his cunning, his intelligence, his fine physical condition all honed to a hunter's perfection, all about to pay off. He was so pleased with himself that he wagged his tail, and in his wagging, thumped against the back of the couch and woke himself from his dream.

Even as he was registering the couch, the darkening room, the wet clusters of snow falling on the far side of the window, and the sound of the radio in the kitchen, he was still wagging his tail, still trying to hold onto the dream. He could smell the rancid fear of the moose, and he knew he'd been only moments away from turning the animal, avoiding a last exhausted kick, ripping into the critical tendons. He could almost feel the crash of the moose onto the snow, the taste of its red-hot blood.

Across the room, the electric heater kicked on—coils glowing, fan whooshing warmth toward the couch. Buck stretched, scraping his feet over the upholstery, shifting his weight until he rolled onto his back with his legs in the air. Ah! The heat felt good. The couch felt good. As much as he was disappointed to wake from such a dream before its climax, he was not so sorry to find himself where he was, amid his creature comforts. The radio played classical music, sweet and low; his person always left it on when she went to work, partly for his entertainment but mostly as a deterrent to thievery. He was glad for this, glad he didn't have to take the entire responsibility for home security—to risk having his neck jammed in a door by some hoodlum, or being shot.

The days-long, stomach-pinching hunger of his dream had faded to an ordinary rapaciousness, and Buck rolled back over and then dropped his front feet to the floor. He stared again out the window—the thick flakes swirling around the eaves, plastering themselves to the side of the collapsing pumpkin on the back porch rail—and took his time dragging his back legs off the couch. He stood in the window, and the breath from his nostrils blew a frosty area in front of his face until all the outside world looked frozen and blizzard-blown. He could just see his chain where it was snapped to its overhead line, and a clean white surface overlaid everything he'd trampled earlier, all his yellow snow.

Buck padded softly toward the kitchen and, still the hunter, crept cautiously to his bowl. Leftover oatmeal, with raisins, formed a mound like a gut pile, and in another second he was upon it, grabbing and swallowing with a fierce, competitive hunger that sent gobs slathering from the side of his mouth onto the woodwork and refrigerator. He licked his bowl clean, licked the linoleum floor. He drank deeply from his water bowl, imagining all the while that he'd broken out the fresh water himself, that he'd found the thin outlet edge of a pond and shattered its ice cover by rearing up and punching down hard with his huge front paws. This was how it was done, in real wolf life, in his alpha dreams.

At dusk, his person took him for a walk in the woods. The snow was old now, the trails packed by hikers and skiers and dogsled teams. Unleashed, he ran back and forth and in circles—chasing scents, kicking up snow, wrestling a broken branch. A startled squirrel dashed between trees, and Buck tore after it, scattering snow in his mad scramble, coming within inches of the fast, flicking tail and then leaping twice his height up the side of a spruce trunk in a last, desperate act of predatory pursuit. His teeth snapped air.

His person, leash wrapped around her middle like a cinched-up belt, laughed at him.

Buck continued to circle the base of the tree, jumping against it as the squirrel chittered and shook its flamboyant tail just beyond his reach. Each time he moved to one side of the tree, the squirrel picked its way to the opposite side; when he circled back around, the squirrel went the other way, so that all he could even see of it was an occasional bulging dark eye, that maddening tail.

His person went on ahead. "Buck," she called. "Buckely-buck, here, boy!" She broke off a stick and threw it along the trail.

He pretended he didn't care about the squirrel or the stick. Nose to the ground, he ran after other scents. A shred of

Tootsie Roll wrapper stopped him for a sniff, and then he kept on. He dove under a snow-crusted bough and sent a shower of white powder all down his back and through the brush. Chickadees cheeped after him.

He looped away from the main trail, and he heard his person calling after him, "Come, Buck, come," and then fainter, and then more demanding in tone but fainter still. He ran through the woods over squirrel and stray dog tracks, past piles of broken spruce cones and the tiny, scratched footprints of shrews, around a stand of birches. He came out of the woods at the edge of a subdivision, paused there a moment to look at lighted houses, to listen to distant barking. Two children were playing on a snow berm in a cul-de-sac, their nylon snowsuits zinging as they flung themselves headlong over the side.

Trotting, he kept to the edge of the woods. Past backyards filled with swing sets and recreational vehicles, he felt again as he had in his moose dream: at ease in his skin, slinky and alive, purposeful. He could no longer hear the call of his person, but listened instead to something more ancient—a pulse, an impulse—that led him forward. He was strong and smart and famished; he knew himself to be the animal above all others, the top of the heap. His broad feet padded easily, quietly, over the snow.

He paused again behind a darkened house, looked at the empty driveway, a crumbling snowman. Packed pathways connected the house to the woodpile, the toolshed, the hutch. He slunk low and breathed hard, felt the fire rising in his belly, made for the hutch.

Chicken wire covered the hutch front and bottom; a littering of rabbit droppings speckled the snow underneath. A pair of small gray rabbits huddled and twitched in a corner filled with straw. They shrunk from Buck and made little, high-pitched squeals. He held them with his eyes. For a minute none of the three moved—not the rabbits, not Buck—and then his back leg—the one he'd lifted and not quite set down again—quivered.

The rabbits pressed against their wall.

Buck attacked. He took on the hutch, its screening, its heavy wooden frame, the hinged and hooked lid. He fought with his claws and teeth, with snarls and foamy drool, while the rabbits thumped their feet and screamed. He ripped staples from the chicken wire, splintered wood, clawed his way under and through the rocking hutch. He got his big head inside, and he chomped the two pet rabbits, wolfing them in bloody pieces, pink ears and hide, meat and cottontail, leaving nothing but a tipped hutch, blood in the snow, a spilled serving of rabbit feed and crisp, frozen lettuce. The taste was ferocious and sweet, fought-for, earned, wildly satisfying.

"Hey!" someone yelled from a neighboring house, and Buck streaked back to the woods. He stood in shadow and gulped mouthfuls of dry snow, watched the door close on a square of orange light, the man disappear again. He trotted farther into the woods and rolled in the snow, back and forth, forcing the clean powder through his fur, wiping his chin, his face, feeling the taut fullness of his belly. Then he shook himself and trotted back, across squirrel tracks, around deadfall, back to the main trail.

His person wasn't far from where he'd left her. He bounded up, gleeful, as though he'd accidentally misplaced her and only just found her again.

"You bad Bucko," she said, but her voice was more relieved than angry. "Where have you been?"

He wagged and pushed his head against her, and she reached a gloved hand into her pocket and pulled out a tiny bone-shaped dog biscuit. He took this from her, with all the daintiness he knew, and crunched it once in his back teeth before he swallowed. As she leaned over to clip the leash to his collar, Buck licked her full in the face. Life was good. Life was rich. The couch, the heater, the music, the dreams awaited, and then it would be time again to eat.

The Woman Who Would Marry a Bear

THE BRIDE-TO-BE sat at her kitchen table with *Brides* magazine, turning down pages and making notes on a pad of paper. There were so many decisions to be made, so many details to attend to. Naturally, she wanted everything about her wedding to be perfect. Suzanne looked in the magazine at the photos of a cherry-blossom wedding, bridesmaids in dotted Swiss and pink butterfly bows. They were heavenly: the armfuls of blossoms, the flower girls with pink cheeks and more blossoms tucked into their golden hair. Her two little nieces were dark, and, to tell the truth, sort of sour-looking, but that was what she had to work with.

She turned down the page with the cherry blossoms and went on to an article about registering for gifts. She would need to choose silver and china patterns. Already, she could imagine them before her, glowing and glittering down the length of a long, cloth covered table. Serving spoons and butter knives, platters and casseroles, linens, candlesticks, a teapot of Japanese design—the gifts she would need to make her new home.

Shuffling and snuffling noises began at the rear of the house. She heard the back door creak, movement through the hall. A bear entered the kitchen and rose up on his hind legs before the counter.

Suzanne continued paging through her magazine.

He was a magnificent bear, six hundred pounds of muscle and gorgeously thick, sun flecked fur. When he stood at the counter, his back to the woman, the fur of his massive back parted down the middle of a dark stripe that ran from the base of his head to his triangular tail. He placed one heavy paw on the counter, pinning a bag of Dorito chips, and tore the wrapping.

"Don't make a mess there," Suzanne said.

He turned his dish-shaped head and nearsightedly surveyed the room. Pieces of chip stuck to the end of his nose the way bits of rubbed eraser stick to an eraser head. His jaw worked slowly, his mouth opening over pink gums and gleaming canines. Then he dropped to the floor and swung his head back and forth, as though sighting down the long barrel of his pale muzzle. His eyes, the color of old wet pennies, turned from Suzanne to the door to Suzanne again.

Suzanne ran a hand through the hair at the back of her neck and sighed. "I've got so much to do. I absolutely must get the invitation order to the engravers tomorrow. And decide on napkins and matchbooks."

The bear walked away, stiff-legged, rolling enormous shoulders. He moved quietly, his claws barely clicking against the linoleum. As he passed through the doorway into the living room, Suzanne stared absently after him and chewed on the end of her pen. She made another note on her pad, examined the polish on one nail, rested her chin on her hand.

A minute later Suzanne sniffed disagreeably. She pushed back her chair and got to her feet, stomped to the cleaning cabinet below the kitchen sink. She knocked around among the floor waxes and oven cleaners, emerging with a can of room deodorizer. This she sprayed liberally around the kitchen, pointing the fluorocarbon-driven drizzle into the four corners, the air above the counter, and the doorway. She covered every scent of food, home, human, and bear with the fragrance of artificial pines.

At the florist's, Suzanne looked in the glass cases and in picture books. Wildflowers, she'd learned, were very popular this year, and that's what she wanted.

"Too puny," she said, looking at yet another example of a wild orchid.

The florist rubbed a finger against the corner of her mouth. "They're smaller than your domestic orchids," she said. "Wildflowers are. They haven't been bred for size and shape. What you get is something more delicate, feminine."

"Droopy." Suzanne turned plastic pages in the florist's selection book. "No daisies. Daisies are passé."

"We could fashion, I think, a very nice mixed bouquet, round and full and still natural looking." The woman fluttered her hands in front of her chest, a gesture that made her look like a pollinating bee. "The wild poppies and orchids will be very nice when they're softened with something lacy."

Suzanne looked dubious. The only thing she liked about the orchids was the idea that someone in a faraway forest was going to hunt them one by one. That was ever so much classier than buying from a greenhouse. She looked again at her list. "I've still got the corsages, the boutonnieres, flowers for the church, and the table centerpieces." She flipped to the white section of the book again. A label caught her eye. "Bear flower!"

"A member of the saxifrage family. It grows only in Alaska and parts of northern Canada," the florist said.

"That'll be my married name. Bear." Suzanne peered more intently at the photo. "Cool—matching flowers."

"We have some in the case," the florist said, going to get them. "I'm sure we can integrate them into your scheme." She placed them on the table, and they looked at them together with some of the other wildflowers. They weren't really all that attractive, in Suzanne's opinion. Too stalky. Still, this was the kind of detail that would make her wedding memorable. People would say, years later, *Remember the bear flowers at the Bear wedding?*

The door to the shop tinkled, and the bear entered, huge and heavy, his weight shifting as he stepped from paw to paw across the front room and into the back, where the two women leaned over the flowers.

"Here he is!" Suzanne exclaimed. "Look, we found something called a bear flower. And it's a wildflower, just like I wanted."

The bear raised his massive head to the counter and thrust forward nostrils like a monstrous, oversized electrical outlet, flaring and shrinking, rimmed with bubbles of mucus. The starry petals lifted to meet his inhalation, and then, as he released his breath, were blown back. He tilted his head and opened his mouth, and the flowers disappeared into the space behind his teeth.

"Stop that!" Suzanne grabbed a roll of the paper used to wrap cut flowers and whopped the bear, hard, across the snout. His head jerked away and the back part of his mouth stretched open so that spittle and a chain of crushed petals spilled out. The fur on the back of his neck and shoulders stiffened, waving like fringe, and his ears flattened against his head.

"Ohhh," Suzanne said, sounding like she might cry. "I

don't know why I bother trying to make everything absolutely perfect." She turned back to the florist. "It's such a women's thing, isn't it? It just takes a female sensibility to care about doing things right, to have any idea about what looks nice." She waved her hand dismissively at the bear. "They have absolutely no *sense.*"

The bear, his head lowered into a corner, opened and closed his jaw with a couple of smacking noises and swallowed the flowers. He shook his head as if to shake off the impact of the paper roll, and the fur on his neck and shoulders relaxed. Still tossing his head, he walked, a little more hurriedly, back the way he'd come.

Suzanne looked at her watch. "Darn. I'm going to be late to the photographer's. Just put the damaged flowers on my bill, will you?" In her rush from the shop she forgot, entirely, to leave her swatches of bridesmaid colors.

Suzanne agreed to have her mother help her plan the reception's dinner menu. The two of them gathered in Suzanne's living room with lists of caterers, foods, guests, decorations, and other details.

Suzanne's mother surveyed her over the top of her glasses. "You *are* sure you want to go through with this? It's not too late to change your mind."

"Mo-ther!" Suzanne brushed back her hair so that it fell over her arm to her elbow, and then she turned to admire it. "We are not going to have that conversation again. You wanted to help, so this is where you get to participate. We need to get a menu pinned down."

"I just hope you've taken everything into account. Compatibility is such a big part of marriage. Your father and I . . . "

Suzanne covered her ears. "I don't need this lecture."

"Well, just listen for a moment. What if, for example, he really loved sports and you really loved opera. You might have a basic incompatibility."

"No way. I hate opera. C'mon. Let's get serious here."

"This is what mothers are for."

"No, it's not. I have it right here." Suzanne waved a glossy book at her mother. "The authors of *Planning Your Wedding* say, and I quote, 'the role of mother is moral support and to do those things that are delegated by the bride.'"

Her mother looked at the closed book. "You memorized that?"

"Or words to that effect." Suzanne took a long swallow from a Pepsi, then set the can back on the table. "I don't think I want roast beef. Then you get into a thing where it's too rare for some people and not rare enough for others, and it's just kind of gross anyway, when they've got a guy carving it up right there in front of people and blood running all over the place."

"Are you sure he, you know, doesn't have any bad habits? What if you find out later he's got some annoying little habit that you just can't live with?"

"Like what?"

"I don't know. Your Aunt Ruth married a man who never slept. He was always wanting to go do something in the middle of the night, or he'd just bang around the house and keep her awake. He wore her right out."

"Not a problem. He sleeps *a lot*."

"Well, that could be a problem, too."

"He snores."

"He snores?"

"That's what I said. But I know what to do. I just won't let him lie on his back. Ever hear of sewing a tennis ball into the back of a nightshirt?"

Suzanne's mother looked slightly scandalized.

"Ma." Suzanne made eye contact. "I got that from Ann Landers." She drained the rest of her Pepsi and tossed the can across the room into an open sack of garbage. She rummaged through her purse for her makeup kit, snapped open her compact, and examined her face. She touched a finger to one mascaraed eyelash.

"You don't want roast beef," her mother said. "What would you like instead?"

"I was thinking of veal. It has such *couture*, it's just so much better looking. Some bright vegetables would go well with it. I want those really light, flaky rolls. And the butter absolutely needs to be those little balls, like tiny scoops of ice cream. Are you writing this down? Then we can call the caterer."

Suzanne's mother started a new list on a yellow pad.

Suzanne, dangling her leg over the arm of the sofa, discovered the beginning of a run in her pantyhose. She stretched and pulled at the material to draw the run up and down her leg, and then she ripped at the hole to widen its track.

"We used to put a little clear nail polish on our runs to stop them," her mother said.

Suzanne pulled back her skirt and stretched the hose to draw the run right up to her hip. "I love to do this," she said. "Did I tell you I decided on my silver pattern?" She fumbled for her magazine and turned to a dogeared page. "Victoria. It's me, don't you think?"

"Whatever you like," her mother said, handing the magazine back.

Suzanne read, "'Sterling gives your table an aura of romance and a sense of heritage.' Not to mention that it's worth a lot of dough." She stood up and stripped off her pantyhose, wadded them into a ball, and stuffed them into the garbage sack.

Her friends, coworkers, and female relatives gave Suzanne a bridal shower. She sat in the center of a cheerful circle and opened gifts as they were passed to her. She attended to each with ceremony, lingering over its unwrapping—pulling apart designer papers and ribbons, digging through boxes of Styrofoam peanuts, unfolding sheets of bubble wrap, sorting through layers of colored tissue paper and bleached white cardboard.

Like buried treasure, each present finally emerged from the depths of its packaging. Lingerie, curling irons, a disposable camera, an electronic address book, plastic recipe boxes, Plexiglas picture frames, an electric juicer—the essentials and delights of married life. Each was passed around to choruses of admiration and approval. Emptied boxes and crumpled wrappings piled higher and higher, filled corners, overflowed the room into the next, then the apartment into the outside hall. Suzanne felt faint with happiness.

They had tea and cakes and told of other showers, weddings, babies, new boyfriends, sales, and the price of red peppers. Someone recommended a place where the bridesmaids could have their shoes dyed.

NANCY LORD

"There he is!" someone said, and they all rushed to the windows.

On the sidewalk below, the bear was walking, the dark stripe down his back shifting from side to side with the sway of his shoulders and haunches. From five stories up, surrounded by concrete and cars, he didn't look particularly large or impressive. The women watched him step off the curb into the space between a new Buick and a minivan and then, when another car rushed past, retreat to the sidewalk again. He stepped slowly, almost gingerly, as though the pavement was hard on his feet. He sniffed at a spindly tree surrounded by a wire fence and then continued past it, head down. His fur, in the shadow of the buildings and against the gray street, looked dusty and dull, colorless.

The women watched and were embarrassed. More than anything, he looked to them like a street person—dull, slow, meandering. Finally, Suzanne's best friend said, "He certainly looks . . . furry."

"He looks very cuddly," another girl said.

"Yes, cuddly!" They all agreed. They went back to their tea and cakes.

<hr />

Suzanne bought a new used car—a big, heavy American sedan with a powerful engine and an oil leak. It got twelve miles to each gallon of gas and needed a quart of oil with every fill-up, but she didn't mind.

Her mother and sister came to help her finalize her wedding plans. They stood in the driveway, and she showed them the car. It started with a varoom, belching stinky black exhaust. She revved the engine, backed the car down the driveway, opened and shut the electric windows, and ran the air conditioner. She made her mother and sister get into the backseat and listen to the tape deck, loud, while she turned up the speakers one at a time so they could hear just what top-of-the-line quality they were.

"It's big," her sister said, when they were standing in the driveway again.

"We'll need the room," Suzanne said. "Family-size. Besides, I want a safe car. Not one of those little things that will fold up like a tin can if you run into something. If I'm in an accident, *I* want to be the one to walk away from it."

They went inside and talked details. Decisions had to be made about housing out-of-town guests and which of the girl cousins would be in charge of the guestbook. Suzanne sent her sister to call the videographer to make sure he knew what time to come. While her sister was out of the room, she showed her mother the gifts she'd bought for her attendants—perfume bottles with real ivory knobs.

Suzanne's sister came back and offered to buy birdseed for tossing after the wedding.

"Are you kidding?" Suzanne made a face. "I'm not having *birdseed* at my wedding. I've already got the pouches, monogrammed and everything, for the rice. This is a class act, you know—strictly traditional. Strictly white rice."

"With birdseed," her sister said, "the birds can clean it up off the walks. When they eat rice, it swells in their stomachs."

"So tell the greedy little buzzards to stay away. This isn't their wedding." She turned to her mother. "Can you imagine?"

"Whatever you like, dear. It's your day."

"Hey!" Suzanne bounced to her feet. "Did I show you the

coffee grinder I got?" She ushered her mother and sister into the kitchen and ran the grinder. She left it running while she demonstrated her new coffeemaker, espresso machine, electric knife, mixer, can opener, blender, food processor, juicer, vegetable slicer, ice cream maker, and vacuum cleaner—one and another, all at the same time, all at top speed.

Outside, the bear stood on the manicured, pest-proofed lawn and listened to the roar. He watched the electric meter beside the back door spin around and around. He paced along one side of the house, turned and paced back. A low growl rumbled in his throat and then he shook his head and made a chopping sound with his teeth.

Suzanne wasn't through. She rushed from counter to table to closet and shelf, plugging in new appliances, pushing buttons, turning switches. She popped popcorn in the hot-air popper, fired up the singing tea kettle, moved the exhaust fan to high. She turned on the radio, the minitelevision, the larger television, and the CD player. Running past doorways, she hit light switches and threw closed-curtain rooms into a blaze of humming fluorescence. In the bathroom, she blasted and whirlpooled a tub of hot water and set the hair dryer, electric toothbrush, and fan going. She snapped, pushed, and adjusted every variety of button and dial until the entire house throbbed.

Finally, she stood taut and trembling in the middle of it all, arms flung fisted into the air. "Yes, *yes,* *YES!*" she cried.

Had the curtains not been closed to keep the sunlight from fading the furniture, and had every electrical appliance and entertainment in the house not been pulsing at top speed, the women might have seen or heard the bear beside the house. But as it was, not one of them noticed him crash through a rhododendron bush and run across the lawn. He ran fast, as fast as bearly possible, half again as fast as any human. His body stretched into speed, propelled by his tremendous muscles and powerful heart. Divots of torn grass scattered in his wake.

He looked back just once, a wide-eyed, wary, hunted look that showed crescents of white at the corners of both eyes, and then he was gone into the woods. He ran into fading light, into deep, soft, far forest, into wilderness.

The wedding was quietly called off.

The Man Who Went Through Everything

NOAH'S IDEA OF LIFE was this: it was a long river, and he was in a canoe going down it. Sometimes the river was flat and smooth, and he didn't have to do anything except glide along and enjoy the sun. Sometimes there were, like rapids, and he had to paddle like hell not to crash into rocks or get washed overboard. The one thing, though, was that the current was strong and his paddle was small, and there was no going back the way he'd come.

He had, in fact, never been in a canoe in his life. But he knew about them. He'd seen them in the outdoor catalogues he collected and on the tops of cars, turned upside down, and once a bunch of them chained beside a lake, like great silvery seals on leashes. He knew they came in aluminum or canvas or fiberglass and could be painted to look like birch bark, which is what they had been made out of originally, when the Indians invented them. He also knew about rivers. He'd thrown sticks and paper cups into rivers on one side of the road and then crossed over and watched them float out of the culvert on the other side, and so he knew about water and currents. He was thinking one day he would build a wheel to turn in the water and give him free electricity, so he wouldn't need to pay for it, but first he would need to live beside a river so the wires wouldn't have to be too long. It was something he was designing, though, in his head, for a time when he might live beside a river.

He knew all the expressions that had to do with his idea of life being like a river. *Go with the flow. That's water under the bridge. You can't fight the current.* He collected these sayings, the way he collected ideas that would one day make him rich.

There was also *Get sent up the river.* This meant, when he was a boy, get sent to a juvenile detention facility. Now it meant get sent to prison. Neither of which he had ever experienced, thank god for that, but it was one more expression. Upriver he didn't want to go.

Lying flat on his back on the mattress that was his bed, in the apartment that had been his for three weeks since the unfortunate incident in his last one, which had been his first apartment after living in the family home for most of his forty-three years, Noah let himself go on, picturing the river that was his life. The river behind him, which he would never see again, was lined with overgrown banks—trees and bushes and twisted vines, what he heard a girl once call shintangle—so that even if a person could paddle upstream, it would be hard to see what had happened there. Whereas, the river downstream was going to go past open fields and nice beaches and the occasional shade tree. There were curves ahead, so you never could see just where you were going, but it was always someplace new and fresh, where you hadn't yet put your feet in the sand and messed it up. Noah had, he admitted, done his share of messing up sand. But then, you couldn't much park your canoe without stirring up a little mud. You had to stop sometimes and leave your mark along that great river of life. Maybe the canoe's got a couple of good dents in it, too. Well, he wasn't drowning yet. His head was well above water.

When he could think of no more river words, Noah got up and checked to make sure his coffeepot was turned off, and then he

NANCY LORD

went out and walked to the Arby's for dinner. He was not driving his van, the Dodge that sat at the curb, because it had about one capful of gasoline left in the tank, and when it came down to a choice between gas or food, he would almost always take the food. Besides, he didn't mind drifting for a while on his river, instead of paddling. Or instead of having a motor on the back of his canoe, which he would never have, anyway, because, for one thing, that would allow him to go upstream and would ruin the whole idea.

It was hard to let it alone, the river thing, now that he'd got it going. He made himself think about his dinner, which would be, as usual, number five with a large curly fries and Dr. Pepper.

Food was the reason he'd lived at home for forty-three years, and food was the reason he'd left. Always there'd been cereal in the cupboard and milk in the fridge, and almost always his mother had cooked some kind of roast something on Sundays. He gave her money, sometimes, when he had it, and he carried in the bags of groceries from the car, and he had made it his job to sharpen the knives. It wasn't like he didn't contribute, never mind what his sisters said. Still, in recent years both his parents had started to drop heavy hints about needing his room for visiting grandchildren or storage, and how inconvenient it was for them to hear him shower at night or to have to pick up his newspapers from the couch, and wouldn't he like more of his own independence? When he ate, his mother sometimes looked at him like she resented every bite he took, but then the next moment she would be plying him with cake and canned peaches. This was because she was unstable.

In the end she got his attention when she tried to poison him.

That was a story all its own, but he thought it sufficed to say that kitty litter is made out of some kind of clay, and it's not meant to be eaten. Beyond that, there was a question about how clean it was or wasn't—that is, whether the cat, Leonard, had already had an acquaintance with it.

At Arby's he ordered his usual and took it home because, really, he liked to watch TV when he ate, even if they hadn't asked him to always take his food away with him instead of sitting in a booth or at a table, after that accidental thing happened with the Arby's sauce and those two girls.

Noah was both an antiques dealer and an artist. In his opinion, this explained a lot about him. It explained, for example, why he had to have a van, even though vans were more expensive than cars and they kept getting taken away when he couldn't make the payments, which of course he couldn't, not regularly, being an artist. But he had to have a van to move his furniture and artwork.

This also explained why he worked at night. Artists work best at night when the creative juices flow. (Yes, like a river, like life.)

After dinner and television, as the lights were snapping off in all the houses and apartments he passed, he walked to his parents' house, which was only a few blocks away and where he still kept his studio in the detached garage at the back end of the lot. There, he turned on lights, space heater, and radio (not too loud) and went to work. First, he had to move things. He restacked chairs onto a table and turned a

NANCY LORD

bookcase around and uncovered another, round table. This was a piece he'd begun on a few nights earlier, starting at the bottom, the curved feet and legs, circling them with bands of colors. Red, blue, green, yellow, then red again. He picked a brush hair off one of the yellow bands. He was pretty happy with what he'd done. Now, he set the thing on its feet and studied the top. It had scratches on it, nothing he couldn't work with. He ran his hands over the surface, letting the feel of it inspire him. He knew, though, already, what he would paint. His favorite artist was Picasso, and he would paint a Picasso, in the same bright colors as the legs, and with a red circle around the rim. He had a book to go by, a library book he'd forgotten to take back and which he was sure they didn't want back now anyway, because it had paint on it and some missing pages. He tore the Picasso from the book and pinned it where he could see it, and he went to work.

His workspace was a little crowded; this he admitted. Twice he tripped over the space heater cord and disconnected it, and one of those times he put his hand in wet paint. To get to the far side of the table without turning it, which he couldn't do without touching the wet red rim, he had to move another line of chairs out into the yard. Yes, he had quite a collection, and this wasn't all. He owned a lot more completed artworks, and many more pieces of antique furniture, mostly spindle chairs, which he kept elsewhere. Unfortunately, he couldn't access them right now because they were locked up. There was a disagreement with the owner of the building about rent, which Noah was sure would be cleared up soon, when the owner realized that as long as the door was locked he wasn't going to get any rent, and then he, the owner, would let Noah come get the stuff and he would move it someplace else, possibly into his apartment.

After a while he took a nap in the overstuffed chair under the window, and then he softened his brushes in turpentine and painted some more, first from the jar of yellow, then of blue, and always looking up at the Picasso and being careful to copy it as exactly as he could.

Sometime in the morning he heard the neighbor woman creak out of her house and cross to his parents' house, where she tapped on the door and then let herself in. When she came back out after a few minutes, she stopped and knocked on the side of the garage.

"Hello, Noah," she said. "I saw your lights."

He opened the door narrowly, until it jammed against part of a bedstead.

She craned her neck in. "I just took some pastries to your mother and father. I'm sorry they're not feeling better. It's a hard thing, getting old. I hope you're looking in on them now and then?" She waited, expectantly.

"Hello, Mrs. Garber," Noah said, as politely as he'd been saying since grade school.

"It smells awful of paint in here," she said. "Are you sure you have enough ventilation?"

"I'm just about done with this one," he said. "Would you like to see it? You can have first offer on it if you like it."

"Oh, you know, Noah, I'm not in the market for any more furniture. I have a houseful. But I'll take a look. I'm sure it's beautiful." She squeezed in and around until she could see the tabletop.

"That's nice," she started to say, and then her voice got very

56

cold. "If I were you, Noah, I'd be very careful who you showed that to." She backed out quickly, and Noah had to shout behind her, "It's Picasso!"

When she was gone, he looked at his masterpiece. It was a good likeness, all angles and bright colors. Maybe he'd made the exaggerated penis bigger than Picasso's, and he'd painted that red barb on the end of it so that, in another sense, it looked like a devil's tail. It was not that he necessarily thought he could improve upon Picasso, it was just that he had his own style. Well, Picasso probably wasn't appreciated in his day, either. Great artists never were.

Later, he went to the woods. He'd found a shack there with a couple of old chairs that just needed to be recaned, and he'd taken them already, but he also fancied the weathered boards on the outside, and he'd come back with a crowbar.

He walked on the dirt road, and there was a teenaged girl in front of him, also walking on the road. "Hello, young lady," he called.

She looked behind her and then she walked faster.

He walked faster, too. He wanted to get the boards, and then he would paint them, or he might varnish them and put hooks on the top so they could be hung outside someone's house, and he would custom-paint the person's name after the person picked out the one he wanted. He had a million ideas like this for making things out of wood and painting them.

He was still banging on the shack, wishing he'd brought some other tools, when the policemen showed up.

They took him in, and he just knew it was for vandalism

again, which he had never committed in his life, but then he found out it wasn't for vandalism at all and not even for theft. It was that girl.

He laughed.

"Why are you laughing?"

"I didn't do anything. I said 'hello.'"

"She said you were following her. With a crowbar. She felt you were stalking her."

"No, sir, I wasn't."

The one policeman looked at the other. "And, besides, we have this previous complaint against you for domestic violence. For beating your wife."

Now they were really mixed up. Noah didn't have a wife, never had, never so far as he knew *would* have, although he wouldn't count that possibility out altogether. He told them this. They obviously had him confused with someone else.

They read him the name. "Funny, she's got the same last name as you."

Oh, his *mother*. His mother wasn't his wife. He never beat his mother, he only pushed her, and it was only because she was old that she fell backwards and nearly broke a hip. She had got hysterical, yelling "I could have broke a hip," and that's why she called the police. He explained it all now to the two policemen. She hadn't pressed charges in the end, anyway, after she wasn't hysterical anymore.

They let him go. The told him not to go back in those woods and not to talk to girls that didn't want to be talked to, but they let him keep the boards and the crowbar. And also, they said when he was walking with a crowbar, it would be better if he didn't keep slapping it against his hand.

There was some song he couldn't remember, it had words about a river: *She just keep on rollin' along.*

At Easter, Noah's older sister invited him for Sunday dinner: salty ham and scalloped potatoes and a plate of deviled eggs made from the colored ones left that morning by the Big Bunny. The meal, down to the peanuts in the silver dish, was the same one his mother had always fixed, only now his sisters were carrying on the tradition. His parents were there, dressed in their Sunday clothes, sunk into facing couches. They were sipping their Easter sherry, and already his father's face had taken on the raccoon coloring that meant that pretty soon he would begin to talk down the Democrats in general and Hillary Clinton in particular. Cheryl, Noah's sister, was doing something with food in the kitchen, and her husband was hollering out the door at their two kids, teenagers, who had escaped already to the backyard. Noah's other sister and her family were late. Noah was not. He had arrived precisely on time.

Noah had on his mind, and had had on his mind for several days, an artistic need. He cornered Cheryl in the kitchen, where she was spilling steaming water into the sink from a huge pressure cooker.

"I'd like to borrow your camera," he said.

Cheryl looked up at him just for a second, her face red and sweaty from the kitchen heat, and he could see in her eyes that she couldn't believe he'd said the thing he'd said. But it was all very simple, the progression he'd worked out in his head. The secret to his success was going to be well-lit photos in a snappy-looking portfolio, and then when he went into a gallery, or anywhere there were rich people, they could see his work and pick out the pieces they liked, instead of him having to drag the pieces around, of which he had too many anyway to do that. It did not bother him that he had never sold a painted chair or table yet. (He *had* traded some). That was not something he thought about, although he did think about a gallery he'd been in recently where the woman told him they didn't deal in folk art, and when he showed her more pictures, she called someone on the phone who he thought for a minute was a prospective buyer, but then a man came and took him by the elbow and led him to the door and through the door and would not look at even one photo, the ignoramus. To top it all off, when Noah got home he found the man had ripped a button right off his sleeve.

"Why don't you not bother me right now, Noah," Cheryl said. "I'm trying to get dinner on."

He had already heard, in his mind, his sister say *yes*, and so he moved away from the sink and stood in the middle of the floor, where Cheryl now bumped into him as she reached for the refrigerator. "I'll bring it back tomorrow," he said.

"Noah," his sister said, and this time he understood that he had not, in fact, heard the word *yes*. "Did you not borrow my camera once before? What happened to that camera?"

"Someone stole it."

"And why did someone steal it?" Her eyes were flinging arrows at him, not unlike Mrs. Garber's in the garage.

"Because they were a bad person."

"Oh, right, *they* were a bad person and you left *my* camera on the seat of *your* van and left the van unlocked in a real first-class part of town."

His other sister arrived then, and her three kids and her boyfriend and her boyfriend's mother. Each of the children, guarding a green-grass Easter basket, was paraded through the living room and kitchen. The little girls wore pink and green flowered dresses, matching, and white straw hats that kept falling over their eyes, and the littler boy, who they called Rocky, had on short pants and a midget's suit jacket. "Absolutely, absolutely," their mother shouted, "no candy before dinner. I will *shoot* the first person, child or adult, with chocolate on his breath." Noah thought she might look at him, but she stormed right by with a bottle of wine in one hand and a corkscrew in the other.

Noah sat in the living room and talked to the boyfriend's mother. She asked him how were things going, and he said *good*, and she asked him was that his van out front and he said *yes, it was,* and she said orange was a pretty color, and he said *did she by any chance need any furniture because he was an antiques dealer and could get her a good deal on chairs and paint them for her, too, if she wanted, orange or any other color or, what was his specialty, hand-painted rings, very labor intensive, but he would make her a good deal.*

His mother said, "This isn't *Tradeo,* this is Easter dinner."

Tradeo was the radio program where you called up and sold things you didn't need anymore.

His father said, "What is that on your face? You trying to grow a hippie beard?"

Noah fingered the silky strands of hair growing out of his chin. They were kind of few and far between, but some of them were two inches long, and he liked tugging on them. He thought tugging on chin hairs made a person look thoughtful.

His father rattled on about something, and the kids flew through the room, and Laurie, his now-all-sweet sister, came in with a tray of olives and celery sticks and passed them around, and then the two teenagers came in, because they'd been told they had to, and sat with crossed arms, and the dog, a golden retriever, came in and swept two sherry glasses and the dish of nuts off the coffee table with one wag of its tail. Somehow this was Noah's fault, because he had scratched the dog's head, or so he was made to feel when everyone said, "Oh, Noah." He was going to clean up, but his mother and father and both of the teenagers were already on their feet, crashing into one another, and his sister Laurie and the brother-in-law that lived there suddenly were in the middle of it all, too, and everyone was picking nuts out of the carpet and sponging with cocktail napkins and pouring more drinks and yanking on the poor dog, and so Noah snuck off to the hall and into the TV room.

In the TV room the younger children were watching a video. Noah watched with them and paged through a computer magazine, and then he looked by chance into one of the Easter baskets lying on the carpet and saw a black jellybean.

"Rocky," he said. "This your basket?"

"This one." Rocky pointed to a different basket.

"Why don't we do an inventory? Find out exactly what the Big Bunny brought you."

Rocky sat with him on the carpet, and they divided the candies into solid chocolate eggs, the bigger eggs with cream fillings, marshmallow chicks, and jellybeans. Sure enough, Rocky had black jellybeans, four of them.

"How much will you take for these?" Noah said, placing the four in his palm.

Rocky shrugged.

Noah looked in his pockets. He had a nickel and six pennies. "Tell you what," he said. "I'll give you one cent for each and a one-cent bonus for being my best customer." He held out the nickel. "Five cents."

Rocky took the coin. Noah jingled the candies in his fist, then popped one into his mouth before placing the others in his breast pocket. The bean, back behind his teeth, melted off its sugar coating and turned rubbery. He did not chew it. He sucked it until it was gone, and it was as good and as licoricey as he knew it would be.

But by then the girls, too, had made their deals. They drove a hard bargain. They took all his money, three sticks of gum, two very good wood screws, a bottle cap he'd been saving because he was quite sure the number on it was one of the rare ones that would complete a set and win a trip to Paris, and the loop off the back of his shirt, which the bigger and harder-bargaining girl got to pull. He also promised them that, when they got older, he would buy beer for them. They snickered at him and said, "Beer! We don't drink beer!"

Dinner was served, and Noah's father got going about Hill and Billary Clinton. Noah ate his dinner and thought about the bumps of black jellybeans he could feel in his pocket, pressing against his heart like points of sweetness. His father kept going, and his sisters and their husbands/boyfriends offered their own thoughts about the state of the country and especially the schools, and the teenagers said school sucked, and then someone asked for *more potatoes please, they are so good*, and they all talked about how much weight they were putting on and they would get more exercise soon, when the weather improved, except for Mother, who was too thin and would see another doctor soon. Noah heard it all around him like swirling, churning water, and he knew he was, for this one day, caught in an eddy and going nowhere.

Rocky said, "Uncle Noah likes the black ones best."

There was a moment of silence, and then his father said, "Black people? When has Noah taken up with Negroes?"

"Jellybeans!" the girls shouted, and then his sister, their mother, said, in a way that was not very nice, *what's this about candy, Noah, you weren't into the kids' candy were you, Noah, have you been eating the kids' candy?*

He was in the eddy, the whirlpool, and it was just about making him dizzy. He knew he could fight it, he could flail around like a wet bug, he could jump out of his canoe, he could get all excited like everyone else and probably drown for it. Or he could just float.

He went with the water, with the flow. He sat tight in his canoe. He rocked in the waves without resisting. Later, he would give himself an extra stroke and get on down the river, leaving this all behind in the shintangle.

Saturday, at the outdoor flea market, Noah strolled up one lane and down the next, looking. When he had the fee, he sometimes had a booth of his own, but mostly he came to the market to look and kibitz and argue over the value of things. Here, more than anywhere, he floated his serene stretches of river.

He pawed through a pile of old rusted farm tools, slid the drawers of a bureau in and out, sat and read a little book about bonsai trees, and talked for a long time to a fellow he knew who had a new batch of wooden dowels from one of the mills. He played with a mechanical bank that the person selling it said was Teddy Roosevelt shooting a bear, where the trigger mechanism propelled the coins through a slot in a tree, and a bear popped up out of the top of the tree. He looked at chairs, of course, turning them upside down to check their construction and right side up to test their wobbles. He found a set of oak stools he liked and tried to barter for them, but the fat man only shook his head and kept repeating the price. He wandered off and came back and got the man's card so he could call him later, and then he looked at kitchen utensils, including what he thought must be the world's largest soup ladle.

He looked at toasters and waffle irons, some with wooden handles, and he saw a coffeepot that made him turn hot in the head. "That," he said, pointing to the offending pot, "is an accident waiting to happen."

The young woman behind the table looked at him quizzically.

"I don't suppose you remember that three-alarm blaze on Elm Street last month," he said. It had been bad enough, coming home to that—his apartment with all its windows broken and everything blackened and wet, but then the fire marshal came to check for arson and questioned him three different times. What kind of coffeepot was it that even if you left it on with no water in it, it would melt its own plastic parts and your counter and then burn up your whole house? His parents had had to get him a lawyer and all that, just because the arson people found burned-out cans of paint stripper in his kitchen and melted clothes he'd packed in garbage bags when he moved, which they kept on calling "flammable rags." That was all river under the bridge now, but it still bothered him. The woman said, "A coffeepot started a fire?"

"Yes it did, that exact model. I strongly suggest you shit-can that before it causes some innocent person a whole lot of problems." The pot, with its black cord draped like a wick across it, was making him exceedingly nervous, so that he was pulling on his chin hairs and the hair of his hot head at the same time with both hands, and he could tell the young woman was getting nervous, too, because she had moved her cash box and was looking around like she wanted to call out to someone. He backed away and got out of that lane as fast as he could, back to the safety of wooden skis and *National Geographic*s and ladies' underwear seconds, all the nice nonelectrical things that could not very easily go wrong, unless you looked at the underwear too closely or for too long.

It was there, past the pairs of white army skis with their cable bindings, that he found the canoe.

It was the smallest real canoe he'd ever seen, just the size for one person. It was made not from aluminum or canvas or even fiberglass but from lightweight plastic, and it was painted in swaths and patches of green and gray and brown, the colors of leaves and mud and dark water. He fell in love with the camouflage and the whole look of the canoe, and with its single shellacked birch paddle.

The man wanted thirty dollars, and Noah got him down to twenty, and then the man threw in a red bandana to tie on the end of it, which just stuck out through the roped-together doors of his van.

———

He launched that same afternoon, from the bank of the river he carried his canoe to from the parking lot at the shopping center where he had stocked up on chips and soda. He got his feet wet getting in, but after that he just sat back in the stern, Indian-style, the way the man had told him, kneeling with his heels under his bum, and he paddled, first on one side and then on the other. Pretty soon he got the feel for how it went, and he stopped crashing into trees that had fallen over the bank and turning too much sideways against the current.

It was a lovely day, with cotton clouds in the sky and birds fighting over nests, and the river made a lot of wonderful swishy sounds. There were a few houses in the distance, across brambly fields, and road noises past them, but mostly it was just Noah and the river, just going along. He could not remember when he had felt quite so right about his life.

After a time, he heard more rumblings, like constant thunderous road traffic in the distance, and after some more time, it came to him both that the noise was getting louder and that it wasn't traffic. He had forgotten that rivers sometimes went over falls, and that the river he was on was perhaps the same one he knew from the city, where Indians had used to camp at the falls and he'd dug through rubble there to find arrowheads. Later it was dammed for power for the mills and still was, with most of the water going over the top and falling hundreds of feet in a big white roaring frothiness.

"I'm up a creek without a paddle," he said aloud, and for another minute he wondered about the logic of this, why an *up* and not a *down*, and then he tossed his paddle overboard, where it skidded over the surface before settling into its own pattern of drifting down the river, slowly turning and falling behind him until it looked like just a pale stick.

Noah lay down in the canoe, which, with his knees flexed and jammed against the sides, he filled end-to-end. He felt the plastic rippling along his back as the canoe made its way through the water, and the cold that seeped into his back. He turned his head so that one ear was against the plastic, and he heard all the swishing sounds amplified. He felt as though there was barely any barrier between the river and himself. He was *of* it, or *in* it, or maybe even *it*.

He drifted on, and the falls got louder and louder. Noah thought about the other Noah, who had boarded the animals two by two onto his ark to save them from the flood. In his canoe he hadn't room for even a chipmunk, which was just as well, because he saw now that he wasn't going to save anything, not even himself. Life was like a river, that was for sure. *Life* would go on. His life—maybe *his* life was like a drop of water in the river, maybe a molecule. Maybe a bird or fish would drink that molecule. The roar of the falls grew louder, and Noah, on the river, soon in the river, was comfortable enough with that idea.

Wolverine Grudge

UNTIL SHE WAS THIRTY-ONE years old, Julia had always thought that a wolverine was a female wolf. This was not, she thought, completely unreasonable. She was a city person; it was not as though her skills at animal identification were called upon that often. There were parallels she could use in her defense: for example, the names Paul and Pauline, Claude and Claudine. A man was a ballet dancer, but a woman was a ballerina.

She would not even have cared, six years after she learned the truth of wolverines, except that she kept remembering that it was Peter—then her boyfriend—who had disabused her of her notion, and that he had done this in a not very nice way. She no longer remembered how they had come, in what might have been a romantic moment, to the topic of conversation, but she remembered very clearly how hard Peter had laughed at her and how bad she had felt. Later she had looked up the animal in the dictionary and found its picture; it was a stocky, furry thing with a bushy tail and fangy teeth, something like a very large, nasty-looking ferret.

There were, in the years of their marriage, many more egregious examples of Peter's cruel behavior toward her, but this one early instance later settled upon Julia with emblematic rankness. Belatedly, she was full of the fury she should have flung at Peter on the wolverine occasion. She was equally wild with anger at herself for not having been smart enough to know that a man who would laugh at her for such a small thing would not be a man with whom she would want to spend the rest of her life. This acknowledgement somehow proved the point (Peter's point) that she really was stupid, and this made her mad all over again.

In normal life, they might have, after the divorce, simply gone their own ways. After all, people got divorced all the time; after the division of possessions and friends, they found new apartments, got the sound systems they'd always wanted anyway, arranged kitchen shelves to fit their own eating habits, and, after a time, found new interests in the love and/or sex department. Julia's and Peter's situation was uncomplicated in the sense that there were no children. (*Except for Peter*, Julia would always explain, drawing snickers from her women friends.)

But life would not be normal for Julia. For Peter, she supposed it was. She lay in bed at night and imagined him with some new, young girlfriend or—which rankled her perhaps more—playing her Bruce Springsteen CD. That CD, which she had owned forever, practically since CDs were invented, had somehow ended up with Peter, although it could mean nothing to him except that it had been so dear to her. The fact that he had it meant to her that he'd never even known what was important to her, or else he'd snuck it into his pile just to spite her. This made her madder and madder and prevented her from getting any sleep at all, which caused her to be drowsy and dull and even more angry the next day at work, where she did particularly poor work and snapped at her coworkers.

Julia worked in the city's planning office and was supposed to think about quality-of-life issues. She could think only about *her* quality of life, which had nothing to do with pocket parks, bike trails, housing densities, or landscaping ordinances. Her quality of life was, as she put it, *shit*.

"Shit, shit, shit," she had said that afternoon in her cubicle.

Her cubicle partner, Angie, had looked up and sighed. "You gotta get rid of that anger," she said. "It's poison."

"Of course it's poison," she said. "It's killing me."

"Well, you gotta get rid of it." Angie looked over her glasses. "No offense, but the rest of us are getting tired of it. We're done with the sympathy. We invited you out after work, we bought the margaritas, we told you he was no good. OK, get over it. Life goes on."

It was true that Angie and others had told her Peter was no good, that they'd never liked him anyway, that she was much better off without him. Which was not exactly what she'd wanted to hear. She'd wasted more than six years with a man who was no good, and everyone had known it except her? How stupid was she, exactly?

The fish on her screensaver swam around and around.

"I can't stand for him to be happy," she said.

"Then make him unhappy," Angie said, and turned back to her work.

She would make him unhappy. She would make him more unhappy than he'd ever been. He had never been very unhappy, which was something that enraged her about him. Even in their darkest days as a couple, he had continued to laugh and to sleep soundly. She would never forgive him for that.

She lay in bed that night and tried to replace her usual maddening visions of him with determined plotting.

Everything she could think of was so obvious; it was the stuff of stalker movies and newspaper headlines. She could leave threatening messages on his answering machine, she could find out who his girlfriend was and kill her cat, she could break into his apartment and go through all his belongings with a chainsaw or maybe just a big knife and a hammer. She could arrange for some kind of accident to happen to him, but really, she wasn't that kind of person. It made her sick to think about what that one woman did, cutting off her husband's little dick and then throwing it from her car window onto someone's lawn. What kind of crazed person could do something like that?

All night she tried to think of something she could do to make Peter royally unhappy, and all night she failed and got madder and madder.

The next day she was so exhausted that she forgot two appointments and couldn't bring herself to even read her e-mail. She invented a migraine and went home early, where she pummeled her couch pillows nearly to death.

What, what, could she do to make that man one one-hundredth as unhappy as she was?

Finally, she remembered a *Seinfeld* episode in which George tried to get a waitress fired by repeatedly calling her at work. George, not being very clever at these things, had not pretended to be other than himself, with the result that *he* was banned from the restaurant, while the waitress quit anyway to pursue a successful artistic career. That was television and that was George; Julia could surely improve upon the concept.

Peter loved his job, which was in the development section of a software company. Julia had never quite understood what it was he actually did; as far as she could tell, the job involved

72   NANCY LORD

playing computer games all day. Every morning, after his night of blissfully sound sleep, Peter dashed off to work with great enthusiasm, and every evening he returned from work cheerful and invigorated, full of exuberance about computer code and his "team," which had had one brilliant idea after another. None of this ever seemed fair to Julia, who everyday dragged herself off to slave over rewrites of municipal ordinances and attempts to appease various unappeasable interests. Her grievances against Peter included the fact that he had too much fun at work, got paid considerably more than she did (nevermind his stock options), and never had to worry about what he wore to his office, where, judging from the holiday parties she'd reluctantly attended, half the staff had green hair.

⁓

The next day at lunch, Julia walked seven blocks out of her way to use a pay phone. She called Peter's company and circumvented the voice mail to talk to a real person. "Tell him," she told the receptionist in a disguised, low-class kind of voice, "that he better call Candy. He knows what it's about."

"Your number?" the receptionist asked, as pleasant as all the rest in that unrelentingly happy office.

"Oh, he's got my number. You bet he's got my number." Julia hung up and smiled all the way back to her office. She could imagine the receptionist writing it down: *Call Candy.* She could imagine Peter, having of course no idea who Candy was, coming back to the receptionist and raising his eyebrows at her, the way he liked to ask questions without actually asking them, and the receptionist saying, somewhat apologetically, "She said you knew her number." Peter could scratch his handsome head all afternoon.

Near the end of the day, Julia took another hike and made another call. "This is Candy," she said, as though she and the receptionist were already old friends. "He didn't call me."

The receptionist wanted to put her through to voice mail, but she wouldn't let her. Instead, she left a number—a number copied from the back of an "alternative" newspaper she'd found in the booth. *Lonely?* the ad asked. For all she knew, there was a Candy who worked at such a place, and she and Peter, if he called, could have a grand old time confusing one another. And if he didn't call, well, she didn't know a receptionist yet who didn't do her own talking. Very soon—possibly within hours— every last soul in Peter's department would know he was receiving calls from a woman of questionable character. They would have to wonder if their buddy Peter was as nerdily stable and safe as they had thought.

Julia was so delighted with herself that she bought a bottle of schnapps and went home and got blitzed. In a ridiculously jovial state, she created an entire persona for Candy—*heh-heh*—Barr. Candy wore tight streetwalker clothes that showed her thighs rubbing together. Candy tripped around in the kind of sling-back high heels that Julia and her friends referred to as "come-fuck-me shoes." Candy chewed gum and smoked cigarettes and had bad, stained teeth. She wore a big gold cross on a chain around her neck and a smeary tattoo of a tulip on one tit. Yes, Candy was a real work of art.

The next morning Julia, vehemently hungover, made another call. She made her voice sound sad. "Oh, hi, honey," she said to the receptionist. "It's Candy again. That man is breaking my

74 NANCY LORD

heart. Will you tell him if he doesn't call me or come see me, I don't know what I'll do? I waited and waited. He's not that heartless, is he?"

The receptionist thought that no, he wasn't that heartless. She suggested Candy call back in another hour, when Peter would likely be at his desk.

"Oh, honey, I don't know. Maybe you could tell me, though, what kind of a man does he seem like to you? Does he seem like someone who keeps his obligations? Like, if he owed for, you know, services rendered, would he pay his bill? Or does he take advantage of people and then, like, walk away?" Julia was so impressed with her act she was, like, almost bringing herself to tears.

"I'm afraid I couldn't say," the receptionist said. "But I'm sure he'd like to clear up whatever misunderstanding there is between the two of you. Would you like to leave your number again?"

"Another hour? I don't know if I'll still be alive in another hour."

Julia had not planned to say this, but now that she had, it seemed the exact right thing. She waited to hear what the receptionist would say.

The receptionist said, "May I take your number?"

Julia hung up. Heartless, heartless. Those computer people, once you cut through appearances, were all as cold as their plastic keyboards.

But, she thought, information works in mysterious ways.

Julia planned her days around reaching various distant phone booths at times she knew Peter would be out of his office. In

THE MAN WHO SWAM WITH BEAVERS   75 each Candy call, she suggested to the receptionist as Peter's problems debts, drugs, insemination, disease, unusual sexual proclivities, and office thievery. A few times Peter was indeed at his desk, and the receptionist put her through. "Hello. Hello? *Hell-o?*" She listened to Peter's voice, so familiar and yet so distant, and didn't answer. Every time she cut off the call, it was like snapping her teeth shut; she thought she tasted blood.

At night, at home, she tried to imagine the developing situation—the talk, the doubts, Peter's own undermining confusion. She would think of these in general ways, but when she tried to picture them in more detail, she always reverted to the moment when he had snickered at her, "Female wolf!? You think a wolverine is a female wolf?" and she once again was made to feel wholly stupid and mad, mad, mad. She could see, then, every detail—the curl of Peter's mouth, his blue oxford shirt, the way he had beat his fist against the couch back in unrepressed, utter amusement.

She drank more and then she burrowed into her unmade bed in the darkened room and spent more torturous nights in black anger. She no longer washed her bedclothes, which took on a musky animal smell, and for need of finding ever more distant and varied phone booths, she no longer had time for laundry or trips to the dry cleaners. She quit cooking and fell to eating crackers scavenged from the back of her cupboards and whatever donuts and cakes appeared at the office. She missed one and then two styling appointments, and her hair grew bushy and uneven and fell into a new part across the top of her head.

She paced her cubicle as though it were a cage, and she snarled at Angie and the others at work, but mostly she was gone, roaming the city in search of phone booths, biting her own bitter anger. At home, exhausted, she curled around herself and waited. She was sure she would at last hear that Peter had been given the heave-ho.

"Julia, Julia," Angie said. "You're a glutton for misery."

When she was told to no longer come to work, she was not much concerned. She hadn't been at work very much anyway, and little that had come to her desk had received more attention than what it took to mound it into a protective barrier around her space. Freed from the interference of her job, she spent her days ranging over the city, marking available phones, placing her badgering calls and generally growling at the world. She no longer saw any friends, shopped, or thought about anything beyond her deep-down, beastly pissed-offness. She didn't much notice or care that Peter's receptionist, after telling her several times to stop calling, now just hung up on her. She shouted at street people and bit one on the hand when he offered her a drink from his bottle. When she no longer had an apartment, she took possession of a doorway and guarded it vigorously; within it, she built her den of cardboard, newspapers, and a fake-fur jacket that she pulled over herself late at night when, sleepless, she spat her fury at all the world. "Naw, naw, naw" became her vocabulary.

"What the devil," a man in a dumpster said one night, jumping clear after nearly losing an eye to Julia's clawing hand. She ripped through bags of decaying chicken and mushy fruit, biting out chunks and scattering the rest.

Gradually, over the next weeks, Julia forgot about *Seinfeld* and laughter and any roots to her motivation. She forgot about

Candy. She no longer picked the black phone receivers off their hooks; instead, she only pulled at their reinforced metal cords. She forgot, finally, about Peter. She forgot that she'd been mad, and what she'd been mad about. She forgot everything except that, somewhere, in her past, there had been something about a wolverine. A wolverine, or particularly a female wolverine, which had belonged to her, or her to it, or something, something that had to do with something with a ferocious kind of need.

What Was Washing Around Out There

A T THE END OF THE DAY, Willis came back from fishing, moored the skiff out front, and rowed ashore in the little dinghy. Altona met him on the beach. "Catch some?"

"Three hundred fifty dollars."

"Kings?"

"Twelve."

His face was another shade browner than when he'd left in the morning and his smell was warm and fishy, that smell Altona had never noticed when she was in fish up to her own neck, but which now, when she didn't go in the boat anymore, didn't smell so good. For a minute she missed the not-smelling-by-being-in-the-middle-of-it, all the years before her legs got their circulation problems, when she and Willis had pulled nets together. It was harder for him now, fishing by himself, though he had become like an Indian in his old age and didn't need so much. He fished when he felt like it and not in the bad weather or always starting at the opening, and he didn't want more than what he caught. These days they got what they needed.

Willis stood at the water's edge, catching his breath from the long row and digging a gnat out of his ear with his little finger. She watched him watch the swallows cutting across the sky, then turn to the rattle of a kingfisher up the creek. It was funny, the way he'd got more like an Indian. When she'd married him, Willis was the kind of jumpy white man who was always doing something, always getting ahead, never just sitting around, and especially never sitting around with a bottle between his knees. She was the Indian, from up on the Yukon, and maybe she didn't know exactly what was going on with her village but could see it wasn't good, people hurting themselves and each other. It didn't take much attention from Willis before she was out of there, wearing polyester and cooking Mexican chili instead of boiled beaver tail. They moved down to the coast, took up salmon fishing with nets instead of wheels, and had, she doesn't mind saying, a good life.

Maybe back then she should have asked herself why Willis wanted her so much. It wasn't just that she was good looking, with her straight dark hair and strong arms. She knew things, or she didn't expect too much. What white woman wanted to live in the bush and cut fish?

Young people, now, were trying to get some pride back. Her daughter Catherine married white, lived in a big house in Fairbanks, worked in a school. She taught bilingual, and her girls—Altona's grandchildren—knew how to do beadwork, to dance the old jigging way. Their whole family went to potlatches and ate steaming bowls of moose stew. Those kids, only one-quarter in their blood, were more Indian than their grandmother.

That was all good, she thought. That kind of pride and knowing was good.

It was easier for women, she thought. Harder for men. Hard for Frank, her son. Frank had grown his hair long and worn buckskin and gone to meetings where he learned to talk angry. He went back to the river where her village was no more and tried to fix up a little cabin. He went to the other villages to find cousins and aunts and uncles, but what could he do there? He could count the dead. He went to Fairbanks and washed dishes and got into a training program for mechanics and quit that and went to Anchorage.

Frank called himself Koyukon and Athabaskan and said he was from the Dena, the real true human beings, and he lectured her, his mother, about her failure to know and respect who she was. Red-faced, he got as impatient as the Scotsman he half was. She did not point this out. He did not want to be Scots. He did not want to even be American. *Cultural genocide. Colonialism.* These were some of his favorite words. He had not even stayed in school, yet he knew these words. He quoted Indian Country law.

What did she know? She knew how to look up words in a dictionary when she had to, when she was too embarassed to ask anyone. She would not ask Frank and be stupid. She would not ask Willis and have him shake his hand like he was brushing away a fly. "Oh, that's just Frank," he would say. She looked up the words. *Imperialism. Sovereignty. Dissolution.*

For the last year and a half, they hadn't heard anything from Frank. Every time there was something on the radio about someone burned up in a fire in an abandoned building, or frozen to death in a snowbank, or beaten and left for dead in some Anchorage alley, Altona's heart went fast and heavy. She was always afraid it would be Frank, dying an Indian death.

She didn't know what she could have done differently. Maybe not have children. Not add to the confusion. She had done what seemed right for herself in her time. Now her children and their children had to figure things out for themselves, in their world, which was different than hers. Better, she thought. She still remembered the signs: *No dogs or Indians.*

Altona looked up at the swallows still flashing around. Willis was bent over, turning down his boots. She didn't know what he was thinking—maybe about dinner, maybe about fish that got away. She pictured him leaning over the boat bow, pulling himself back and forth along the corkline like a spider on its strand, ready to pounce, to bundle the big fish in web and hug their thirty or forty pounds up over the side, into the boat. Willis liked nothing in life better than catching kings, though he'd once said that curling himself around her on cold nights was a close second. She imagined him pitching those fish off onto the tender, checking weights, getting his ticket and a cold soda from the fish buyer.

When he straightened up, she took the lunch box and rain jacket out of the dinghy, and Willis dragged the little boat up over the sand.

"Reds?" she asked.

"Forty."

"That's good."

They went into the cabin, and Altona started slicing potatoes. Willis washed his hands and arms, scrubbing away fish slime and silvery scales and the gray aluminum boatstain.

Three hundred fifty dollars—that was good. Not what they used to make, when salmon were worth more. Before the yen lost value, before the Japanese got a taste for beef. Before salmon farms took over the market. Before they began to feel the squeeze from the sports fishermen. Altona knew about all these things. She and Willis read the salmon marketing reports aloud to one another and felt helpless before the pictures of Japanese shoppers and the charts with their plunging lines. Willis went to the cannery office every spring and came away with more sad stories about pack left in freezers and bankruptcy filings.

They ate potatoes and eggs, and Willis told Altona that the whole day, while he worked his net, seismic boats ran lines back and forth in front of the river, setting off explosions and shooting geysers thirty feet high.

"What did the fish think?" Altona asked.

"They didn't like it."

The seismic testing, they both knew, would tell the oil companies what was under that part of the inlet, and by next summer it was entirely possible that oil rigs might be punching holes in their fishing grounds. Willis, though, was not one to get mad about it. He'd even stopped by the big seismic ship a few days earlier and given the men a package of smoked salmon strips. The way he figured, it was better to get along with your neighbors than to fight with them, because you never knew when you might need them. If he got into some kind of trouble someday fishing alone on the flats, he'd want one of those boats to look out for him.

Altona picked up the binoculars from the table and looked at something white on the inlet. She handed the binoculars to Willis. "What's that look like? That white thing."

Willis looked. "Want me to chase it?"

"Does it look like a skiff?"

"Too small." Willis was still looking. "Should I go get it?"

"Up to you. It's a long way off."

"Might be something good."

The way he said *good*, Altona knew he'd already decided to go. He never could resist rip picking. Some of their favorite and most useful things—her big oak cutting board, the aluminum boat hook, plastic totes, and wooden pallets—had come from the rip, where currents brought together whatever was washing around. All their lives they'd never bought a new buoy, just painted their own numbers on ones they collected out there.

Altona hobbled back down to the beach with Willis and watched him drag the dinghy back to the water, row to the skiff, and head off north, shirt flapping. She sat on a rock that caught some of the last sun spilling over the top of the bluff. The warmth went right through her, into her bones. She laughed out loud, remembering the winter before, riding in Catherine's car in Fairbanks and getting a hot seat. She'd thought the engine or something else underneath the car was on fire. She'd jumped out. She'd never heard of a car with electrically heated seats.

She took the binoculars from her pocket and followed Willis, the flat water cleaving before his bow, the orange buoys in the boat bottom visible as the boat planed. He reached the white object in just a few minutes, and she could see that he was right—whatever it was, it wasn't so big. The light was doing that, lifting everything off the water, making it seem bigger. The headlands to the north were doubled over themselves and the mountain, streaky with snow, stood huge and wavery against the pale sky. Still looking with the binoculars, Altona went from one distant oil rig to the next, watching the way they shimmered on their pod legs, the drift of their smudgy exhaust plumes. Frank had worked once, briefly, on a rig. She'd thought the work with chains was too dangerous but, still, she'd been glad to have her son so near. She'd never been too sorry that he'd left fishing. It wasn't what he wanted, and even then she'd known the beach wasn't a place for an angry young man to make his future.

When she lowered the glasses, she couldn't see the skiff or the white object anymore. The tide was drawing it all away. When she focused again, she found the skiff turning in circles and other dark objects—tree trunks and root balls—and peaky waves. Willis was going around and around, looking.

Altona's thoughts drifted back to the seismic boats and their blasting. She knew the oil industry brought money to the state, but she had a hard time thinking much good about something that intruded so much on her life. She suspected the industry was behind the visit from the anthropologist who'd come along the beach out of nowhere the week before.

That young man, in his new leather hiking boots and carrying a walking stick, had bounded right up to her while she'd been doing a wash. He'd spoken broken English, the way they talked in cowboy and Indian movies on TV. "My name Morrison," he said. "I want you tell me old ways, old stories of your people."

She'd been embarrassed for him, talking like that. She'd answered him in normal sentences, apologizing that she wasn't from the area and didn't know any of the old ways and stories. She explained that she was from the interior and had grown up, summers, at a different kind of fishcamp, but she didn't know much from there, either, because she hadn't been paying attention. She kept saying, "I'm not the one to ask, go ask the old people." Fifty-nine was not so old.

He seemed to think, nonetheless, that she knew things it was his job to learn. He ran his little tape recorder and scratched in his little notebook when she told him about her village and family fishcamp on the river, and how she'd learned to cut fish from her mother and grandmother. He asked, did she know any stories about Raven or Crow? About the creation of the world? She knew her Bible stories, knew Genesis, knew what they'd all learned at the village church, but that wasn't what he wanted. She apologized again for having so little to tell him, although it seemed that the things that were so fashionable to know now were the very things she'd been made to feel ashamed of as a child. She gave him a strip of fish from the smokehouse, which he photographed and then ate, tearing at it with his teeth like it was something fierce and raw. At last she remembered a story her grandmother had told, about a little girl who chased a butterfly into the sky and then couldn't get down until an old woman wove a rope and lowered her through clouds. He looked pleased with this and kept pressing her to tell him what it meant. She had no idea what it meant except what seemed obvious. Finally, she told him she guessed it was a story to teach children not to wander too far from home. He wrote this down, his tongue sticking from the corner of his mouth. In the end, he thanked her again and again for all her time and help and had her sign some papers, and he promised that she would be paid a fee as an elder and tradition bearer, like she was some kind of expert.

Whatever it was, she'd guessed he'd got what he wanted. The oil industry had to do things like that, studying who and what was in a place before they went and changed it. That was the law.

Willis was in the rip a long time. She could just barely, with the glasses, see the skiff, its bow turned in one direction, then seeming to head back, then turned again into the rip, the aluminum reflecting sunlight like fire. Closer in, a seal bobbed up,

NANCY LORD

went under, bobbed up again. Flocks of seagulls flew south just inches over the water. Seagull races, Willis called them—the way lines of birds winged by hour after hour, always the same distance over the water, always the same flapping speed. Always heading south. All summer long the flocks flew only south, and it was Willis's idea that the gulls actually flew around and around, in a circle, like horses on a track, down the inlet, then inland and up behind, over the flats and forest, then down again, the same birds over and over, in seagull races.

She looked for the seal again and couldn't find it, and she looked up and down the beach, scanning for the bears that liked to walk past in the evening. There were two young ones this year, light-colored brown bears with upturned noses, that passed almost every day, searching the tideline and gobbling the spawned-out hooligan that washed up. They were as fearless as only young bears can be, and curious enough that whenever they noticed the boat bucking on its mooring or Altona on the porch, they stood up on their hind legs and looked amazingly like muscled young men, arms held fisted at their sides.

Altona moved from her rock to another to catch the last triangle of sun that reached the beach.

At last Willis headed in, bow pointed squarely for shore. He came in past the big boulders and ran the skiff right to the beach. Altona looked into the boat, over the piled net, the anchors and buoys, the oars. He had not washed the boat well. Fish blood and scales were still stuck to the aluminum. Fish smell, ripening, clung to the web and the burlap fish covers. In the boat's center, Willis had piled his treasures—a broken pallet, a couple of seine corks, a thick plank with twisted bolts sticking out.

"What was the white thing?" she asked.

"Dead beluga," Willis said. He heaved the pallet from the skiff. "But there was something else, too."

"What?"

"A dead body. Dead a long time. I'm going to go down to where that seismic ship is and tell them. They got a crane on their boat. I wasn't going to try to pull it in here. I tied some detergent bottles to it so they can find it. It'll be with the beluga. They'll both float down together when the tide turns. Or they can call someone on their radio, troopers or someone."

Altona heard it all, the way Willis laid it out like that, all so factual, but her brain had seized on the first three words. Whose dead body? People died all the time in the inlet, even people they knew. But they'd never found a body before.

"A man?" she asked.

"A man."

She couldn't help herself. "Not Frank."

Willis almost smiled. "No, of course not Frank. Not anyone we know. Like I said, kind of bloated. I didn't look too close. Gray in the hair. I don't know, might have fallen off a boat."

Altona knew most fishermen who drowned fell overboard when they were peeing off the stern. They were half-asleep or maybe drunk or the boat just took a wave they weren't expecting. They fell in and no one saw them go. But men fell off of oil rigs, too, or out of rafts on the rivers and got washed down, and once a tourist lady jumped off, purposely, one of the big cruise ships. Skiffs swamped, and a person got so cold so fast there was no holding on. Could be murder victims got dumped in the inlet, too, washed right down from Anchorage.

"White or Indian?"

Willis just shook his head.

"What kind of clothes?" she asked.

Willis threw the plank out. It fell onto the sand with a heavy smack. "Just regular. Suspenders." He dragged the pallet and the plank above the tideline and started to push the skiff off the beach.

"I'm coming with you," Altona said.

He pulled the skiff back in and helped her over the bow.

It was a long way to the seismic ship at the river. Altona sat out of the wind on the aluminum rail that separated the fish bins from the stern. In the roar of the outboard at full throttle, she and Willis didn't talk. Instead, she thought that if there were 600,000 people in Alaska, there was only a very small, tiny chance that any one dead person would be someone she knew, and a much tinier one that it could ever be Frank. Still, her heart hadn't quite calmed. Frank never wore suspenders. That's why Willis mentioned them. Willis wanted her to be as sure as she ever could be that Frank was safe, just as he, himself, wanted Frank to be safe. He wanted Frank to be other things, too, like smart, agreeable, committed to something he would actually finish. Willis, of course, wanted his son to be at least something like himself.

She tried hard not to think about the dead body washing around in the rip, and so she thought instead about the dead beluga. The last few years, they'd been finding more and more dead whales. She wished she knew what was killing them. Maybe it was pollution, all that crud from the oil rigs, or the poisons flushed out of Anchorage. Maybe it was the seismic booms or not enough to eat or atomic dust falling out of the air or people shooting them. White people weren't supposed to shoot whales, but Native people could kill them for food. More and more Native people were moving to Anchorage from other places where they'd hunted whales, and now they were all hunting that one group of inlet whales. Frank always said, Native people know how to keep in balance with the environment, but she thought Native people would shoot the last whale just as surely as they'd drink themselves to death, and she didn't know whose fault any of that was.

Just then, she remembered a story she could have told that anthropologist. She did know a story about Crow. It was one she knew from when she was a little girl, and she'd used to tell it to Catherine and Frank, too. Crow and Whale both lived on the river, and Crow tricked Whale to make him get stuck in the mud, and then Crow sat there on his back and ate him until there was nothing left, just a pile of bones. And that's the reason there're no whales in rivers anymore, only in the ocean. Whale and all Whale's relatives got mad and stayed away.

When she used to tell this story to her children, they laughed at the idea of a bird eating a whole whale. It was after that when everyone went around saying, *I can't believe I ate the whole thing.* That always made her think of Crow and Whale, until she'd forgotten about them altogether.

The seismic ship, huge and white, was moored in the bay, still in full sunlight. Willis eased up next to it, and Altona gimped forward to wrap their bowline to a cleat. Willis tied the stern tight and then climbed to the deck, where he greeted some men and was led away, presumably to the cabin and the captain. Altona sat in the bow and waited, jerking with the skiff as it tightened and loosened against the side of the ship.

A man in the blue cap of the seismic company came to the rail and offered her a can of Pepsi, dropping it to her with a gentle underarm toss. His face was the color of trout flesh, and his clothes were newer and cleaner than any fisherman's. His voice, when he spoke, was syrupy, like the South.

"We really appreciated that squaw candy your husband brought us the other day. That was really nice of you."

She knew what he meant, of course. She knew what they called the strips of smoked salmon her people had always prepared, up on the river, down here, anywhere salmon had been lifeblood. She knew the ugly word that had traveled across the whole American country, meaning Indian women, meaning their sex. Even as the shame, then the anger, boiled up through her, she knew that the one man before her hadn't meant to insult her. He hadn't even heard himself say that word. She looked not at him, not at the grateful pink face at the rail, but out toward the inlet, to the lower rip into which the dead man and the dead white whale would wash when the tide turned. The man at the rail did not know, she thought, what message Willis had brought. He was as innocent as a man could be of what was washing around out there, of the damage he and his kind had done and continued to do, of his ignorance.

She made herself look back toward the man, and she said, "We have a lot to share." The can of Pepsi was cold in her hand. She opened it and took a long, thirsty drink.

Willis came back, and the dead man in the rip was no longer their responsibility. They motored home with the still-flooding tide. Willis set her on shore and she watched while he took the skiff back to the mooring and began to row in again. It was as though no time at all had passed since he'd returned from his day of fishing, except that they were in shade now and the air was cooler, and the gas tank was that much emptier. Swallows swooped overhead, and a single crow, hopping across the steep, sandy bluff, sent down a pinging slide of dirt and dust. Altona sat on a rock that still held some heat, and waited.

Behold

Here's the scene: Time. 1984—a year, despite the portent of literature and never-ending prophecy, of no great significance. America was halfway through Reagan's rule, in a fever of military spending and neo-anticommunism. Gorbachev had not yet come to power in the Soviet Union, and *glasnost* was not part of the diplomatic vocabulary. On a worldwide scale, I was probably no more or less popular or understood than I'd been for centuries. People prayed to Me, cursed Me, used Me as a justification for their wars.

It's no joke, being the Big Guy, the one people look up to as the Lord, God Almighty. A reputation like that, you get called on a lot. At this time I'm speaking of, much more important, dramatic, and deadly events were taking place than what I'm about to tell you. Nevertheless, for ten days in the fall of 1984, through no fault of My own, I was involved in one particular international incident that might not have turned out so well.

Place. Forget about Moscow and Washington. Find instead the edge of the earth where the two then-superpowers come closest together. A land bridge once connected the continents here and was, in fact, the pathway by which the Americas were first populated. But that's another story. Today fifty-seven miles of water separate the mainlands of the Russian Far East and Alaska. The political boundary between them divides a pair of islands, Big and Little Diomede, not much more than a stone's throw apart.

In the beginning was a routine voyage. A ship, a World War II vintage landing craft, carried supplies from south-central Alaska up the west coast to some seismographic ships doing oil exploration work in the Arctic. The vessel was skippered by a young man, William, all of twenty-five, though he looked much younger. His crew of four was similarly young. Boys, really. On the way back, after successfully completing their delivery, they departed from their course and turned west to travel between the Diomede Islands.

The five young men on the ship, besides the fact that they worked together, had one thing in common. They were all very religious. I make no judgment about this, other than to observe that their piety was somewhat unusual to find on a ship, among young American men, in this period of history. They carried Bibles, and they read and believed them word for word, as fact. They attributed everything good in the world to Me. They looked to Me for everyday guidance in their own lives. I should be flattered. In the ship's galley, they hung a calendar with Bible verses. The reading for September was, proverbially, *The mind of man plans his way, but the Lord directs his steps.*

Crossing between the islands, somewhere near the international dateline, they spotted a gray ship farther to the west. The boy-captain steered toward it while the crew readied a bag of candy. Often before, when they met with Japanese ships on the high seas, they stopped to exchange greetings and toss over a bag of treats. Such acts of friendship warmed their Christian hearts.

They didn't even know the ship was Soviet until its soldiers, armed with machine guns and daggers, leaped onto their decks.

General chaos took over for a while, the Soviet border patrol bewildered by the approach of the smaller boat, William and his

94

crew frightened by the strange language and wary faces. William held up a piece of paper and a pencil, shouting for someone to speak English. Officers on the other side demanded to see the captain. They could not understand what such a ship was doing in their waters, manned only by a handful of pink-faced boys. The bag of candy was dropped and forgotten.

You must understand this: the Americans, in this case, did not have a solid understanding of world history, geography, linguistics, culture. Only the cook, who had attended a Bible college, knew of the Iron Curtain, had a sense of Communism as being opposed to religion. None of them could have told you what the Cold War was or outlined on a map the shape of the Soviet Union. They might have heard Reagan refer to "the evil empire." They'd seen Rambo in the movies and World War II films on television. They had no real idea who Lenin was, had never heard of Chernenko. William—despite being a licensed skipper, savvy in the ways of the sea and in reading nautical charts—had left school in the ninth grade.

"Gestapo!" the mate yelled out.

The Americans were frightened, but they were also angry. They knew the law of the sea: the captain is the master of his ship. "They can't do this!" they shouted as the Soviets disconnected their electronics. "Get off my ship!" William yelled as he and his crew were herded onto the aft deck. When they saw that no one was going to listen to them, they turned toward one another and huddled, arms around each other's shoulders, heads bent, and asked for My help.

I would have liked to have helped, but what could I do? Can I correct the faults of the American education system in two seconds, or overcome the influence of a hundred bad movies? Could I undo the Cold War? If I knew how to make people be nice to each other, I would have done that a long time ago. The first thing I would have advised was, for My sake, don't make a big, noisy, ostentatious show out of praying. Even common sense, you'd think, would tell them that would only freak out the guys in the green uniforms.

~

The Americans prayed, and the Soviets searched the ship. They seized the logs and charts, inspected the electronics, looked into the cargo holds and the crew's quarters. With covetous eyes, they examined William's oldest frayed jeans, now dumped on a corner of his bunk, and his Japanese camera. One soldier held Walkman earphones to his ears, not quite daring to put them on, and heard American rock and roll. He was careful not to smile, which might have looked as though he were enjoying it. In the galley, another opened the microwave oven and looked inside. Everything American was so small. He said to his friend, "How can it be any good, so small? How can you bake bread in such an oven?" He shook boxes of dry food—such small packages, and light, insubstantial as chaff. His friend turned pages on the calendar. It was curious to him, the photos of flowered pathways, candle flames, scripted letters. He commented under his breath, it was like something for old ladies.

The officials studied the chart, saw the ship's course drawn in pencil, the small Xs marking intervals of time. The pencil line extended all the way to Big Diomede, the island forbidden not only to all foreigners, but also to Soviet civilians. The officials scratched their heads and were puzzled. They radioed for instructions, for help, someone who could speak English. They

NANCY LORD

opened their briefcases and searched out the correct paper-work. The reports that would have to be filed! They began to fill them out, noting coordinates, the name of the American ship, and how it had made its approach—steaming up over the eastern horizon. So boldly! For what possible reason?

The Americans took up their Bibles, opened them ran-domly, as though they would find answers there, as though the Bible was a Christian *I Ching*. They read aloud a passage about an olive tree, and this cheered them. They were sure that I would see them through. In fact, it came to them that perhaps I had something in mind for them that was very, very big.

Two more Soviet vessels arrived, one with an English-lan-guage interpreter.

"We demand to be released," William said to him.

The interpreter—Ivan—turned to the official in charge and repeated this in Russian. The official's head went back and his lips parted over gold teeth. He was most definitely amused.

"That is not possible," Ivan said in crisp British tones.

"Then we'll escape."

"That is not possible," Ivan said again. Although the American spoke not at all clearly, and with a nasty temper, Ivan was grateful for the opportunity to speak with any Americans at all. Normally, his job was to translate documents, mostly of a scientific nature, and the chance to actually speak aloud, and perhaps to pick up a few new American idioms, was very appealing to him. He sat straight and kept a pleasant face.

"You can't do this to us," the mate said. "It's not legal. We've got rights."

The official placed paperwork on the wheelhouse table, indicated where William was to sign.

"No way." William folded his arms across his chest. He spoke to the rest of his crew. "No one signs nothing. That's an order."

Ivan studied William a minute before he turned to the official. They talked for several minutes. The official removed sheets of flimsy gray paper from a folder and placed them around the table with pens.

"You will write the answers to these questions," Ivan said. "Name, address, your work, purpose to be in these waters."

Each member of the crew wrote down this information. Purpose: freight hauling.

"Now you write your name."

"We're not signing nothing." William pushed his paper into the center of the table. The others did the same, jaws clenched tight.

Ivan asked, "Why do you make this so difficult?"

William asked, "Do you believe in God?"

"It is not for me to answer your questions. I am only inter-preter."

"Do you?" the mate demanded.

"I am atheist," Ivan said. "I have no need for . . ." He could not immediately think of the word for *crutch*. "It is not for me to talk. You must answer the questions." He stubbed his finger against one of the papers.

William said, "I ask you to open your heart to Jesus Christ, and He will save you, too."

That is how it happened that the American ship was towed to the Soviet mainland and the captain and crew were taken to a barracks in the port of Provideniya. Confined to a room in which the windows were papered over from the outside, deprived of their valuables, including their Bibles, they rejected the bowls of soup brought to them, the pickled herring, the hothouse cucumbers, and the rich dark bread. They were prisoners, after all, prisoners like—they told each other—the apostles Paul and Silas, beaten and held in stocks until a great earthquake broke open the prison door and the jailer fell down before them and asked to be saved. "It happened to them. It could happen to us," the cook said. They refused all food, accepted only tea, and put their faith in—Who else? Me. I'm supposed to make an earthquake pop open the door? They got down on their knees and prayed that their families would know where they were.

"We are here for a reason," they said.

⁓

For three days the captain and crew were brought, sometimes one at a time, sometimes in pairs or all together, into a separate room where a series of officials questioned them. Ivan was always present, interpreting. What are your names? For whom do you work? What was the nature of your work in these waters? Why did you cross into Soviet waters? The Americans answered, sometimes orally, sometimes in writing, but they denied crossing into Soviet waters, and they refused to put their signatures on any paper, whether it was prepared by the officials or written by themselves.

Ivan looked at them sadly. He was translating all day long, from early morning until late at night. He was not getting enough sleep. He did not like to be in Provideniya. Provideniya was, for him, not an interesting town, no match for Magadan, the regional center grown out of labor camp headquarters, which is where he lived, and, of course, nothing at all compared to Moscow, which is where he wanted to live. During the height of the Cold War Provideniya had been home to thousands of troops, but most of that was gone now—the troops and the tanks and missiles—and the barracks buildings and warehouses were mostly empty, crumbling. The town was distinguished only by an indoor swimming pool, closed for repairs, and a small brewery.

The latest high-ranking official threw up his hands and stormed from the room. Ivan did not bother to translate his profanities. The military and the KGB—they were not accustomed to such defiance. For what? To get some necessary paperwork filled out? It was embarrassing to them to have these boys refuse, over and over, something so simple as a few questions. It was not an occasion they wanted their subordinates to witness, and it wasn't something they could explain to their superiors. And the Americans—everything they didn't like. They were offended by the hot meals that were brought four times each day, better than Ivan himself got at home. The toilet was not to their liking. They complained bitterly to him about it, and the mate broke the seat out of a perfectly good chair to make a sitting arrangement. The guards had told this, snickering, to Ivan. "Like women!"

Ivan lit another cigarette and asked again about America. Every chance he had, he asked questions from his own curiosity. He wanted to know everything about America. "How many rooms in your flat? How many people? Is it hard to find a flat?"

William and his crew did not know the meaning of *flat*. To them, flats were the short, half-pound cans salmon were packed into. But they figured out that Ivan thought they lived in apartments, and they were amused by this. Who wants to live all crowded together? "Smiley," they said, for this is what they'd decided to call Ivan, "you can take your flat and shove it."

"Shove it?" Ivan asked.

"Stick it," the cook said.

"In your ear," one of the others said.

In truth, though, the Americans liked Ivan. He could talk to them in their own language, and he had a kind face. He wasn't that much older than they were—thirty-one, though he was balding. They knew he had a wife and daughter and went cross-country skiing in the winter. They were quite happy, for the most part, to tell him about their homes and families, cars and trucks, their proud American lives.

"Freedom," the cook said. "We are free to live wherever we want, go wherever we want. Big houses. Many rooms." In actuality, the cook lived in a cabin in the woods, without running water, but that was his right, too, to save money, since he was home so seldom. He wanted Ivan to know the usual American way. Growing up, he'd lived in a big house with his parents.

"How much," Ivan said, "a coat like that?" He pointed to William's nylon jacket.

William shrugged. "I don't remember. Money's no object."

"No object," Ivan said. "How much those athlete's shoes?" He liked very much the running shoes all the Americans wore, leather shoes with stripes and thick, cushy, patterned soles.

The Americans compared shoes among themselves. The mate argued for Nikes. The cook swore by his high-top Adidas. "About fifty dollars," William said.

Ivan whistled. "How much money you earn in a month?"

"Depends."

Ivan could not get any of them to tell him how much they earned. He switched to books, mentioned some American authors he'd read. Steinbeck. Hemingway. Updike. The Americans' looks were blank. He asked, "Do you know Jack London?"

"Guy with a wolf," one of them said.

The mate said, "Do you know Jesus Christ?" His eyes were so staring, like a zealot, that Ivan had to look away. These five were not like anyone he had ever read about in a book.

In their room, between cups of tea and interrogations, the Americans reasoned this way: at least they could talk to Smiley. The way he looked when they mentioned Jesus Christ, they were sure he was ashamed, he wanted to believe. There was a little crack there through which they might reach him. And if they reached him, if they got him to accept the Lord, who knew what else was possible?

On the fourth day, the cook was driven to the ship and allowed to take food from it. Afterward, they feasted on bowls of Cheerios and Frosted Flakes and prayed for additional signs. Being allowed their food was one sign, they decided. They would be able to keep their strength up, as prisoners and—they were not afraid to say—as apostles. To make up for the confiscation of their Bibles, they prayed more often than before and talked aloud about their faith.

So sign the damn statement already, I wanted to shout. Was it too much to ask?

The next day, Ivan wore a suit and tie, and what hair he had shone as though it were freshly washed.

"You're looking pretty spiffy," William said.

This was another new word for Ivan, and he made sure he understood it correctly. "Spiffy," he repeated until he was sure he would remember. "I am very spiffy man."

"Why?" they wanted to know, they who were looking not so spiffy in their same clothes and without recent showers. "Why are you so dressed up today?"

"This evening I go to visit lady."

The Americans looked around at each other, then back at Ivan. "What lady?"

"Lady friend. I go to see her at her flat."

"And do what?" The mate was indignant.

"You know. We eat dinner. She cook a nice meal. We have a pleasant evening together. You know." Just thinking of the woman made Ivan smile, though the Americans—every one of them—were looking scandalized.

"Smiley!" William's voice was half an octave high, his eyes blazing like fire. "What do you mean? You have a wife."

"My wife is in Magadan."

Right there, at the table, the Americans clutched at each other and began to pray. Ivan lit another cigarette. He heard some of their words condemning him for the sin of fornication, asking Me to forgive him.

I know, it was not nice of Me, it was not benevolent, but I had to laugh. Picture this: the passionate Americans, heads bowed together, gripping each other in their righteousness, Ivan rolling his eyes to the ceiling and then purposely blowing smoke at the bent heads.

Ivan rose from his seat and walked out into the hall, where he offered a cigarette to the guard. "All my life," he said, "I've wanted to smoke a Lucky Strike or a Camel, and when at last I have a chance to meet Americans, they don't have cigarettes, they don't smoke. It is a sin, too." The guard leaned against the wall. He, too, was tired of standing all day, waiting, being given triumphant looks by the Americans when they passed. "I don't know," Ivan said. "Is it possible five people can have the same sickness in the head?"

In another room, not far off, a dozen officials consulted, spoke on a telephone, pored over reports. They could not agree who the Americans worked for or for what reason they'd crossed into Soviet waters. They could not believe that Americans ran such a slipshod business. But mainly, they could not, as much as they tried, figure out a way to release the young men until they had given complete statements.

The Americans prayed in even greater earnestness. They prayed for a miracle. The earth should crack open and deliver them. I Myself should appear, as before Moses, and lead them from this wilderness.

"We're here for a reason," William said.

"Prepare the way of the Lord. Make his paths straight," intoned the mate.

They sung out, altogether, "Hallelujah!"

On the sixth day, a guard came for William and led him through the building to a small room. There was a desk and chair in the room, and a phone, the receiver lying on the desk. The guard indicated to William that he should pick up the receiver.

"Hello?" William said.

A woman's voice, sounding very far off, addressed him by name. "I'm with the U. S. Embassy in Moscow. We want you to know that we're doing everything we can to get you released. Are you all right?"

"Yes," William said. "We're OK. Do our families know where we are?"

"They know. We're in contact with them. We'll let them know you're all right. We're doing what we can to get you released. Hang in there."

"Roger." William's eyes filled with tears. "God bless you," he said, but the line had gone dead.

When he burst back in on the others, he was shouting, "It's a miracle! It's a miracle!" Clearly, they reasoned, their prayers had reached their families, told them where they were. They were convinced I was listening—not only that, but that they were in My hands, I would see them through. Even Moscow was in the act now. They redoubled their prayers.

I can tell you, I laughed until I cried. I should have even the power to dial a phone.

The Americans, for all their jubilation, noticed that Ivan seemed troubled. They took this as a good sign, a sign that he was questioning his lack of faith, preparing himself to accept My word. But there was not much time.

They decided the way to reach him was with a letter. This would give him something to keep even after they were gone, something to read and study. The cook wrote it out on a sheet of the flimsy gray Russian paper, a very personal Christian letter. He said he felt a certain connection between the two of them, that he had once been a sinner, too, but that he had opened his heart to God, and that his new friend could, too. It was difficult, trying to get the whole message onto a single sheet of paper, but the cook told the others that he doubted he had ever written more important words in his life. He implied that they might, someday, even be looked upon as some sort of document, not quite a new book of the Bible, mind you, but just imagine—if Smiley took it to heart, became a Christian, passed it on to others. This was quite a responsibility, to choose just the right words!

When the letter was finished, the cook folded it into a tiny square that fit in the hollow of his palm. The next time he was called for questioning, he answered the same questions about who he worked for, what his job consisted of. When the questioning was over and he once again refused to sign the paper placed in front of him, they all walked to the door—the official, the cook, Ivan. The cook turned quickly and pressed the letter into Ivan's hand.

Ivan read the letter through carefully. *You only need to open your heart to the love of Jesus Christ. I was a sinner, too, but today I walk with Jesus. . . . He will show you the way and give you peace.* Dutifully, he then turned it over to the officials. It was a long, cramped, repetitious letter with a lot of abstract words, and Ivan was afraid he'd be made to write out an entire translation. The officials, however, were only interested in the signature. In fact, they were quite excited about it. This paper was a statement of sorts, was it not? Could the signature be legitimately attached to the other papers? Could one name suffice for them all?

For his help, Ivan was given two hours off, and a car and driver. He went to see his lady friend. He tried to tell her about the
cook's letter, the odd obsession of the Americans. It wasn't that
he didn't understand religion, he said. His mother was a deeply
religious person. It gave her comfort to light a candle, to believe
in a greater power. But he did not believe. It was not his nature.
If he believed in anything, it was in literature, but even then,
when he read Tolstoy, he skipped over the preaching. "It's not so
different," he said, pointing out the window at a slogan painted
on the side of a building. *Glory to the Workers.* "It takes a blind
belief. If you don't have that, does it make you a bad person?"

His lady friend, though, was not a philosophical woman.
She was a practical woman, entirely corporeal, and she did not
want to waste time on a discussion of good and bad.

Meanwhile, in the headquarters room, the officials argued
the issue of what constituted an adequate explanation and signature. They paper-clipped various sheets together to see how they
looked. They changed the order of the pages, putting the letter
first on top, then on the bottom. Well, yes, this was stretching the
procedure. Yes, but what other options had they? They did not
want to be holding U. S. citizens. They did not want to be stuck
in a Provideniya barracks for the rest of their lives.

The Americans kept up their prayers. They sensed that things
were going very, very well. They had it figured: as the chosen,
they only needed to pray for guidance, and then be ready for
My signs. They agreed they would watch Smiley. They would
be able to tell from the way he acted what influence the letter
was having.

In the late afternoon, when they were all taken to the interrogation room again, they went expectantly. Ivan was already there, smoking.

"I see you haven't given up cigarettes," William said.

"Should I?" Ivan smiled. In fact, the cigarette was recalling for him the very satisfying pleasure of his *last* cigarette, smoked at that very supine and perfect moment back at his lady's flat. Each inhalation brought it all back to him: the simple, satisfied exhaustion, the smell, the feel of her skin. He lingered with the memory now, the expression on his face one of perfect bliss.

That is what the Americans saw—Ivan's perfect bliss. They could barely contain their happiness for him, for their success, for the future of the Free and Christian World.

A new official strode in and took a seat. He and the Americans looked each other over, and then he began with his questions. They were the same questions as before, but there was something different about this man. The Americans had noticed that he had more medals and bars on his uniform, and he was older, with gray hair. His eyes were deep set, like an ascetic's. William touched his hand to his right earlobe. This was his sign to the others that things were going well. The others nodded to him.

This time, instead of asking, "Why were you going to Big Diomede Island?" or "Why did your chart have a line to Big Diomede Island?" the man placed in front of them a map showing the islands and asked, simply, through Ivan, "Show me, please, where was your course."

William studied the map. It was a straightforward map, just the outlines of the islands, the international dateline between them, some other latitude and longitude notations. He

NANCY LORD

looked at it and then he looked to one side, at the surface of the bare wooden table they'd sat around for so many days. There, in the shine of the old wood, the same spot he must have looked at a thousand times before, he saw worn grooves that looked very much like a cross. The more he looked, the more certain he was that a definite cross—two perpendicular lines, one longer than the other and cut off at the edge of the map—was being presented to him, where it hadn't appeared before.

"Here," he said, tracing his ship's route between the islands. "We meant to put in here." He pointed to the village on the west side of the small island.

"And you went too far this way?" the man asked, dragging his finger just across the line. "You made a small error?"

"I guess." William looked at the others, saw complete trust in their faces.

"Why did you wish to go here?" the man said, now pointing at the village. "It does not seem to be on a direct route to your port."

William watched the cross. When he blurred his eyes a little, he could easily make out, in the worn grain, the outline of the Savior, head fallen to one side, bare and boney feet nailed to the cross. He felt a great sense of peace.

"We had extra time," he said. "We decided to stop to buy some souvenir T-shirts."

In Ivan's translation, this came across as "souvenir underwear." The official and Ivan looked at each other. The official said to Ivan, "What do you think? Am I supposed to believe this?"

Ivan shrugged. "I believe it."

The official looked again at William and the others. "Our imperialistic neighbor sends five boys to the edge of the world to buy underwear. We spend more than a week to find this out, and I have to come all the way from Moscow? I will sign the necessary papers." He pushed back his chair and strode from the room. Nobody saw his flicker of smile as he passed through the door.

"What did he say?" William asked.

"He said he wished you'd brought some cigarettes from that great country of yours, but a pair of nice American athlete's shoes would be a good souvenir, too."

A few hours later, the American ship was under tow, heading east. Onboard, the five Americans shouted *Hallelujah* and *Praise the Lord* until they were hoarse. They broke into their stores of food for Pop-Tarts and prayed some more.

In Provideniya, Ivan wore his new tennis shoes to the airport. They were a size too large, but he liked them very much just the same.

"We sowed the seeds!" William shouted off his deck. "Let the word go forth from Smiley!"

"Praise the Lord!" the others chorused.

The cook punched his fist into the air. "We did it! God gave us a mission, and we brought Him glory! We helped save Smiley's soul!"

Glory-smory. It's not enough I put oxygen and hydrogen together and made things grow, created an earth with trees and butterflies and pistachios, a place fit for the human race to come along and enjoy? I'm supposed to be sending envoys and saving souls?

But as I said, it all turned out OK in the end. In Provideniya today, the door on the old barracks swings open and shut, squeaking in the wind. Over in the main part of town, Russian and American children gather in a schoolroom and sing a song together. *Let there always be sunshine. Let there always be blue sky.*

Let there be, indeed. I said it once before, but I'll say it again: Let there be light. And I'll say something else, repeating Myself again, but maybe this time someone will grasp the meaning and the possibility a little better. *Behold, they are one people.* This is only the beginning of what they will do, and nothing that they propose to do will now be impossible for them.

The Baby Who, According to His Aunt, Resembled His Uncle

I was that baby. I was named Maynard Perry Johnson-Hart, after my parents (hyphenated last) and my two grandfathers (first and second). I know my name sounds like it belongs to an old man, a fact which may also have colored my aunt's thoughts. Had I been born a girl, I would have been named Mary Elizabeth, after my two grandmothers. This was all part of coming from an equal-opportunity home that believes in honoring women and men alike. But an additional reason for my very male name, I understand, is that my parents wanted me to feel comfortable in my masculine identity.

I'd say that after all these years I've grown into my name some, though I still prefer Tor, which is mostly what I've been called since the beginning. It's a Danish name, I'm told, related to Thor, the Norse god of thunder, but if you look it up in a dictionary, you'll find out it's Celtic for a pile of rocks on top of a hill.

Currently I'm fourteen years old.

My family believes in telling the truth about everything to everyone, babies and strangers included. We have no secrets. We don't try to protect anyone's feelings. We just blurt things out. Like this: I just said, "Yo, Ma, you look exactly like a stick of melting butter." She was wearing like a jogging suit, only more elegant, and yellow, and it didn't exactly become her. In this case, I get points both for honesty and figurative language. And then I say, "Mom, you must be losing your mind, because you told me to be home at six and here I am, and now you don't know why you wanted me home. Maybe you should take that new test they've got for Alzheimer's."

The important thing here, aside from my acute honesty, is to know that Ma and Mom are not the same person. When you have two mothers and they both want you to call them equally affectionate names, you get into these kinds of situations having to explain yourself. *That was Ma who drove me to school. Mom's the one who goes to her library job early so she can be free to coach soccer. Yeah, Mom's the one with the long braid. Ma's the one with the sister who lives on a ranch in Wyoming and is married to the guy who . . .* Pretty soon I'm telling the whole story about how our family might or might not be related and explaining genetics, which is a pretty cool science. You know, you don't have to go back very far at all before you find out that everyone's related to everyone else. It's a fact that most of our human genes match exactly and there are only a few that control our differences. We all have the same two eyes about halfway down the head, nose, mouth, similar patterns of male baldness. You get your odd people sometimes like with six fingers or toes or three breasts or weird hereditary diseases that make albinos or giants, but mostly we all look alike. That's aside from skin pigmentation, which simply has to do with whether our ancestors came from places where they needed protection from the sun or not. It's so weird to me that people make such a big deal out of whether someone else's skin is black, brown, white, yellow, or red, and by the way, American Indians were called redskins only because some of the first ones Europeans met had painted their faces with red clay.

⁓

I have two mothers who are lovers. When I was little, the hard part of explaining this was the second part, *lovers*. Two mothers my kindergarten friends could understand. They knew what one mother was, and they knew how to count, one, two. No big stretch there. But *lovers?* What do kindergarten kids know about sex? I explained: they sleep in the same bed. They kiss. They love each other so much they got me.

I got blank looks.

Later, they came at me with questions like *OK, which one's the daddy?* And I had to explain that my mothers weren't, like, butch and femme. They both looked like women. They both *were* women. It wasn't like one went to work and the other stayed home and wore an apron. Like one had hairy arms and the other painted her toenails red. I had to explain a lot about feminist politics and culturally ingrained sexual stereotyping. Not in those words, but that's what it amounted to.

Sure, I got teased some. But things were mostly pretty cool, because Mom and Ma were cool. They took me and my friends camping and to look for dinosaur bones. They brought cupcakes to school when it was their turn—the best kind of cupcakes, swirly-colored inside with chocolate frosting and jimmies—*and* they decorated them with tiny whistles and other gender-neutral toys. They rode bikes and went down hills fast. We had a big backyard, and anyone could come over and mess around on the jungle gym or with lacrosse sticks or dig in the compost for worms. They took us fishing, too, and they'd stop the car if there was something interesting dead by the side of the road so we could look at it. They made the best Halloween costumes, and they knew everything about computers when other parents were still saying, *Duh, what is a hard disk?*

I was still confusing my little friends, though. I could see their minds clicking behind their furrowed brows. *OK,* they would say when they thought they'd figured something out. *Are you adopted or, like, what?*

So then I would explain, like, no, I'm not adopted. I grew in my mother's uterus, the same as they grew in their mothers'. And not that it mattered, because I'd learned very early that adopted children belonged to their families as much as biological children and to talk about them in any other way was a form of discrimination. I did not tell my friends, at least at that stage, that in fact Ma had had to legally adopt me in order to be my legal parent who could visit me in the hospital and sign my field trip permissions and things like that. She had been forced to do this because of how fucked up our political and judicial systems are and how rampant homophobia is in our culture, and there was no other way, in the eyes of the law, that I could have two mothers with equal rights. Later, with my friends, I could get going on this, but not then, although I know my reticence was contrary to the full disclosure policy of my household. *I* knew the truth, but it was hard to explain.

Of course, then they thought they really did get it. Some of them almost smirked. *So really your Mom is your mother. And your Ma is her girlfriend.* And I'd have to explain all over again that, although the egg came from Mom and I grew inside her and was given birth by her, my mothers were equal mothers in that they made the decision to have me together and did the whole pregnancy thing together and were in the delivery room together holding hands and breathing and pushing. (I have the video.) They loved me equally and had all the same parental rights to me. Obviously, I would say, they couldn't *both* have grown me inside their separate bodies, or I'd be two people instead of one. Sometimes choices have to be made. *Right?* Mom's the one who got to have me because, they decided between them, she had the wider pelvis.

This sometimes got us into a thing about twins, of which there were some in our school. I would explain about one egg or two, and if it was two eggs the two babies were the same, genetically, as any two brothers or two sisters or brother and sister. Other times, I had to explain about Caesarian sections. Icky-icky, no one wanted to hear too much about that kind of surgery, though they also had a hard time picturing themselves squirting through a hole between their mothers' legs, down in that mysterious region where the number ones and twos came from. For most of them, the whole birthing business was pretty icky.

The next thing my friends got smart enough to ask was, *ok, if your Mom doesn't like men, how did she get a man's seed inside her? What man put his seed there? Who's your real father*, they squealed, like they'd cracked the case after all. *Who's your REAL father?*

Mom does like men. Mom and Ma both like men, but that doesn't mean either one wants to have sex with them. They don't reject men in particular, only piggish men and the oppressive patriarchy. They actually have quite a few men friends, both gay and straight. But they didn't want sperm from any of them. They didn't want anything emotionally complicated. They wanted parenthood all to themselves, which meant anonymous sperm.

Which is where the sperm bank came in.

The sperm bank is this place, kind of like a money vault, that refrigerates sperm until women who need it come buy it.

The vials are numbered and the numbers are coded to information about the individual sperm donors—nationalities, physical attributes, special talents or interests. A lot of information, actually. Ma and Mom filled out a form with what they were looking for in a donor, and then some computer, like a dating service, spit out their matches.

This is, as my parents say, a whole lot more scientific and sensible than what most people do to make babies.

Now, though, comes the complicated part. When I was born, Ma's sister, who lives on a cattle ranch in Wyoming, came to help. She's married to Roy, who is this hearty Scandinavian type, and it happens that the two of them—my aunt and Roy—look quite a bit alike. This is another curious thing, that people will frequently choose mates who resemble them physically. That is, blond people are attracted to other blond people and tall people to tall people. You know how people look like their pets? It's the same thing. There's a psychology of it called narcissism, and it has to do with an attraction to self, which is not necessarily a bad thing even if it sounds a little funny. Somewhere in our evolution there must have been a good reason for it, to keep people together in their tribes or something. I would like to make more of a study of this, myself.

So Roy and my aunt look alike, and my aunt and Ma look alike because, of course, they're biological sisters, and then the physical characteristics that Ma and Mom shopped for at the sperm bank were ones to match Ma, because they wanted me, their son, to look something like both his parents—not because they had some big ego thing, but just because they thought it would be easier for me. Do you see where I'm going with this? Since I was born bald, and Roy is getting that way, and since I had an old man's name, it's not unreasonable that my aunt took one look at me and said, "My God, he looks just like Roy."

The thing that's just a little unusual is that Roy once went to agriculture school and what the guys at agriculture school used to do for beer money was to go make deposits at the sperm bank.

This is the story of why I look like my uncle, who could possibly be my biological father, although none of us will ever know because the records are sealed and none of us wants to know anyway, although it seems we want to know everything else. Someday my aunt and Roy might have children of their own, and if they do, they'll be my cousins, except they could possibly be my biological half-siblings as well. If Roy is not my sperm donor, then they'll be my cousins without being biologically related to me at all, not that we know of, except in the way that we all are related eventually. And not that it really matters, because family is family regardless.

I would like to work out the numbers, but I don't know where to begin. I don't know how many sperm donors there are or how many deposits they make, on average, or how many children result from them. I did see a television show, though, about a guy whose sperm resulted in three hundred children, and there was a scandal, not because of the number, which Mom and Ma and I all agreed was excessive for any one person, but because he had a genetic kidney disease he was passing on, and even when the sperm bank found out about it, they refused to ditch his sperm. This was not the same sperm bank that my parents used, and the sick children on the TV didn't look much like me, so I'm not too worried about getting a kidney ailment, but I'm hoping that Roy didn't also sell a million vials of sperm, because what if I grow up to be a narcissistic person and fall in love with a woman who looks like me? She could turn out to be my half sister.

Sometimes I lie in bed and think about this and how complicated life can be. I wonder if Roy is my biological father and, if not, what the person who is is like. I wouldn't mind if Roy is because I like Roy, although I've only met him three times in my life. He jokes around a lot, which is important to me, because I want to be funny, and it would really help to have that in my genes. When I was younger, I used to think about playing catch with Roy, throwing a baseball back and forth in a field, and what big muscles he would have in his arms. Sometimes now I think about working on the ranch with Roy, bucking hay bales or whatever it's called, getting all sweaty and itchy and then leaning on the hay wagon to tell dirty men's jokes.

Here's one joke I know: How come it takes just one egg but millions of sperm to make a baby? Because the sperm won't ask directions.

Other times, though, lying in bed, I don't much like the idea of working on a ranch, and I also stop worrying about the numbers and the odds. I think about how there are 5.8 billion people in the world and how amazing it is that, though we all go back to a few common ancestors and we all look pretty much the same, basically, there's such an incredible variety of us in how we think and act and what we do. There are all kinds of pretty terrific people out there, and I really don't think I'm going to have that much trouble finding the right person to love and have sex with and maybe make babies with. Although, I know, it's going to be a challenge to do as well as my Mom and my Ma, who are more than terrific themselves, though this is something I've never actually told them, just as I've never told them about wanting to play catch or buck hay with Roy. Some things are harder to talk about honestly than other things, and it's pretty near impossible for a fourteen-year-old kid to tell his parents that he thinks they've set the absolute high standards for love.

White Bird

IT WAS DECEMBER, and dark. The cabin that belonged to a cousin was located on the north side of a hill, and the sun at its midday peak cleared the rise just enough to appear as a cool yellow light in the front window. Snow had finally come, laying a lumpy white blanket over the yard, and every night hoarfrost grew like feathered mold atop the snow surface and around every twig. The sun never warmed enough to soften the knife-edge constructions, and the wind hadn't blown for days, and so the frost thickened in crispy layers, higher and higher and wider, balanced on crystal points. Now and then, when a cold current passed over the hill, or a chickadee touched down on the crown of a wild celery stalk, a slice of icing broke loose and collapsed into a pile of fine white dust, and the air rang with tinklings, chimes, and cymbals.

The woman, Celeste, came out of the cabin, pee jar in hand. It was late in the morning, and the south sky was a pale streaky calico, citron and gray and blush colored. Celeste was newish to the north, most recently from L. A., where she had had her own cable television show, *Celeste!*, featuring her prophetic and healing abilities. It was through her show that she had met Freddy. She had, in fact, a whole large fan club from K., where the villagers had altered their educational television satellite dish to receive *Celeste!* The show was a call-in show, and the people of K. had called in every day from the one village phone, and she had heard in their softly cadenced voices a very deep, very ancient wisdom. When they invited her to visit, she hardly thought twice before catching the next plane. And then she had met Freddy. If a person existed with greater powers than her own, it was Freddy.

There had been jealousy, and one thing and another, in the village, and that's why they were living now near another town, in a cabin belonging to one of Freddy's many cousins.

Celeste crunched over the yard, the warm pee jar gripped hard in one mittened hand. She was a large woman, and with a knitted afghan draped around her, she looked quite like a slowly moving couch. Her hips shifted one way and the other over her city boots as she tried to avoid either sinking backwards into the punctures made by her stiletto heels or sliding downhill on slick leather soles. At the side of the clearing, where the snow already was burned by yellow holes, she unscrewed the lid and dumped the night's comingled liquids. The snow sizzled and the air smacked with colliding ions, all the hip-hop energy of Freddy's and her mixed pee soup.

It was then that she saw the bird. It sat on a fencepost, huge and blocklike and white, whiter than the snow, shiny even in the dull light, a white like vinyl. The tremendous white beak was nearly half the size of the bird, and it was open wide, exposing with each panting breath a blood-red lining and flickering tongue. Coarse frosty feathers stuck out around the beak like a cat's whiskers, and the eyes were dark and darting rubber bullets. Every white wing and tail feather fell crisply in line, sharp enough to cut wood. The bird shook its hulking shoulders, adjusted its feet on the post. On each foot, each of its three forward-pointing toes was adorned with a ring, each ring with a large colored stone: emerald, ruby, sapphire, amethyst, moonstone, and lapis lazuli.

"Now that is something," Celeste said under her breath. She turned and made her way back to the cabin, and she looked back just once before she closed the door. The bird was still sitting on the fencepost.

Freddy was lying in bed, smoking. His blue-black hair fanned out around him on the pillow, and his eyes were full of sleep.

Celeste stood at the foot of the bed. "Raven was white, right?"

"When?"

"That story you told me. Raven was pure white."

"In the beginning, that's right." Freddy took another drag of his cigarette. "He turned black when he flew up a smoke hole. He got all black from the soot, and he stayed black ever after that. My grandmother told me that story."

"But he was white again? Another time?"

"No. He was always black after that."

"What did you tell me about when the Russians came? I thought he was white then."

Freddy took a deep breath through his nose and stretched his head back. The cords in his neck tightened. "The old people said when the Russians came, they thought it was Raven coming, the original white Raven. It was the sails. They saw the white sails of the ship far off on the water, and it looked like Raven."

"Well, honey." Celeste bent over and grabbed one of his big toes through the covers. "I do believe your ship's come in."

Before Celeste and Freddy met in K., they already knew each other in their dreams. Celeste had dreamed of a slight, long-haired Indian man who moved like water and wore a silver killer whale necklace, and Freddy had dreamed of a woman with webs between her toes. When she'd gotten off that plane in K., they'd recognized each other immediately, and they'd gone to his house and not come out again for four days. For all her psychic powers, which she considered substantial, she'd known at once that she'd met her match. She hadn't been a bit surprised when Freddy told her he was a shaman.

She'd gone back to L.A. only long enough to close up her business, and she'd committed herself now to combining and nurturing their gifts. She knew she could always make a good living helping to find lost belongings and missing persons, or advising in general, or going back on cable, but she wanted more than any of that to concentrate on Freddy and his talents. To this end, they had come away to this cabin in the woods, and Freddy did not have to work repairing snowmachines, or answering phones in an office, or stacking nets on a boat—all of which he'd done before—but only to be quiet and wait and dream. A shaman needs time to dream, because wisdom comes from dreams, and so they had, both of them, spent long hours in bed, and she was the one who cooked and carried in wood for the stove and emptied the pee jar.

And now Raven had come.

Freddy scrambled around amongst the covers and a pile of clothing beside the bed and got himself dressed in long johns and a hat with earflaps.

"No, it's not albino," Celeste said. "It's not like that. You'll see. No, it's not a snowy owl. No. It's not a ptarmigan." She didn't know what a ptarmigan was, but she was sure it wasn't one. It was no ordinary white bird. "Just wait. You'll see." She had a feeling in her bones that the bird wasn't going anywhere. It was going to sit there and be looked at, every last sparkling ring.

They went out on the porch, and Celeste pointed to the bird on the post. "See? I'm not crazy."

As smooth as flowing water, Freddy lowered himself off the edge of the porch to stand on the snow. His huge insulated boots, unlaced, gaped open around his skinny calves, so that he looked like he'd been planted into buckets, and he stood as still and stiff, too, as an ornamental tree. He made a *cluck-chuck* in the back of his throat, a sound like calling chickens, and the bird shuffled its feet around and cocked its square head. He did it again, and the bird hunkered and then launched itself from the post, spreading its enormous wings like sections of silk parachute. Within the pattern of white feathers there were additional patterns—circular designs like epaulets on each shoulder and rounded tabs of light that followed the wings' curvature. Celeste clutched her hands against her chest and sucked in her breath.

The bird landed on the ground, not far from Freddy, and folded up its wings with a crisp, crusty-sounding efficiency. It began to peck at particles of ash and chaff, hopping one way and another. Its feet, thick and horny, embossed the layer of frost with clear, detailed impressions—the scaliness of spread toes, deep toenail pricks, the smooth bands of its rings.

Freddy made more sounds in his throat, catchy *kh* sounds, something like the beginning to a hawking of phlegm. The bird raised its head, dropped its oversized jaw, and repeated the sound. Freddy pulled in his chin and made another back-of-the-throat noise that was like stones falling into water, a hollow echoing that seemed to leave expanding circles in the cold air. The bird made more hawking noises, its perfect white chest rising and falling.

Celeste exhaled. "Holy shit. You got the real thing." She unwrapped the afghan from around her and passed it down to Freddy. "Throw this over it."

"How come?"

"You think if Jesus Christ walked into my yard with a crown of thorns I wouldn't latch onto him long enough for people to know about it?"

And so it happened that the white bird was captured and put into an airline dog kennel that the cousin had stored in the back shed. Celeste fed it green grapes and popcorn through the wire screen. She watched it when it slept; although the white eyelids sealed tight, the eyeballs dodged back and forth underneath them like dark shadows. She concentrated all her energy but only knew that whatever was going to happen was very, very big. For Freddie's part, he let Celeste believe that he talked to the bird, and that the meaning of what was said between them was more than hawking and dokking and glugging noises.

The next morning they drove away in a rattley-bang pickup truck, the dog kennel with the bird in the back, and headed to the city.

Things were busy in the city. Cars sped along the ice-rutted streets, past blackened snowbanks, and exhaust hung in the roadways like fog. Colored lights flashed everywhere, up and down and around the sides of towering buildings. Rough music oozed out of open basement doorways. City ravens with untidy feathers perched on the edges of dumpsters and picked over a carton of smashed eggs in a parking lot. Men in a steamy alley passed a bottle back and forth, back and forth.

Celeste and Freddy checked into a hotel, and Celeste got on the phone to arrange a press conference. Freddy took a long, hot shower, sampling each of the miniature soaps, shampoos, conditioners, lotions, and breath fresheners, and then he wrapped himself in a thick white hotel robe and ordered room-service steaks and fries. He gave the bird all the fries it wanted, with and without ketchup, and he lay on the huge bed and clicked back and forth through thirty-four television channels.

Celeste was still on the phone, still calling the press.

Later, she went out and bought Freddy a pair of leather falconer's gloves. She bought herself a pair of sharp scissors. As a girl she'd helped her Arkansas uncle clip the wings on a peahen to keep it from flying into a neighbor's apricot tree.

❧

At the next day's press conference, Celeste wore a long, diaphanous gown that swirled around her like ten-foot waves. Her hair was piled on her head behind sequined combs, and her metal earrings, which resembled wrecking balls, swung dangerously with each of her flourishes. Bracelets clanked up and down her arms, and she fluttered her ring-decked hands before her bosom like a constant swarm of flies. That morning she had wrestled the emerald and lapis lazuli rings from the knuckled claws of the white bird, on the theory that four was enough for the bird to make an impression, and to see what special powers the rings might confer upon her own self. The gemstones tossed prisms of sealight into every corner of the conference room and across every news-hardened face.

Freddy was dressed in jeans, a clean T-shirt, his killer whale necklace, and his beaded deer-leather vest, a gift Celeste had given him for his birthday. The hotel soaps had made his forehead break out, and so he also wore a baseball cap pulled down to his eyebrows. The cap said *Four Season's Honda,* and the tips of his ears stuck through his hair on both sides, where the cap pressed against his head.

Celeste explained the bird to the assembled press. "Raven made the world. He's like God. You could say he *is* God. Freddy's grandmother told him all sorts of stories about Raven, about how Raven made people out of clay, made rivers and lakes where he spit, things like that. In the beginning he was white. We believe—Freddy and I—and Freddy, you understand, is a shaman—he has very deep spiritual abilities and insights—that this is a supernatural appearance with great significance."

Freddy, wearing the gloves that looked like cooking mitts, reached into the kennel and brought out the bird. He set it on the table, where it hunkered its belly flat to the surface. Camera flashes lit up the room, and the bird only blinked. It was a sorry-looking bird, not nearly as white as it had been in the snow. It had been sitting on newspapers and in filth, and its breast feathers were dingy and stained. Dried ketchup dirtied its chin, and half of its feather-whiskers were bent into crooked angles. Its clipped wings and its posture made it look even more boxy than it was, and its feathers were all so disarrayed that it was impossible, especially under the glare of artificial light, to even see the circular patterns, the epaulets and tabs, on its shoulders. Its eyes had turned dull and were somehow smaller, slitted.

"Is it alive?" someone shouted.

"Of course it's alive," Celeste said. "You can see it breathing." Its mouth sagged open, and its sides moved lightly in and out. "Freddy, see if you can get it to talk. Lift it up so they can see the rings on its toes."

The cameras flashed again, and the video recorders whirred as Freddy lifted the big bird and held out its feet. A crust of bird poop came loose from one of the rings and fell to the floor. Freddy chortled to the bird, but it only hissed from the side of its mouth.

"These two were talking like crazy the other day," Celeste said, "It sent chills up my spine, I'll tell you, it was so clear, the quality of communication that was going on there. You'll have to forgive a little stage fright right now."

The reporters took their pictures and asked questions like, *how much does it weigh* and *what does it eat* and *has a veterinarian been consulted about whether its oversized bill is a deformity.* They began to snap their notebooks closed and to leave, and Celeste caught a few of them in a corner by the door to tell them about her cable show and her psychic and healing powers, and she took a wrist afflicted with carpal tunnel syndrome in her hands and wouldn't let go until the wrist's owner admitted he could feel heat penetrating the muscle and the nerve.

Freddy sat on the edge of the table and petted the bird in his lap.

Later, in the hotel room, the three of them watched themselves on local news. The bird was described as *unique* and *unusual* and *culturally significant.* Celeste and Freddy drank a bottle of champagne. They tried to clean ketchup off the bird with wet washcloths, and they dried it with the bathroom hair dryer. Feathers fell out all over the place, exposing patches of yellow plucked turkey skin.

The publicity worked. The next day Celeste closed deals for White Raven T-shirts, White Raven coffee mugs, White Raven key chains, White Raven refrigerator magnets, and White Raven totem pole pencil sharpeners. There was also talk about a line of cosmetics and movie options. The day after that, Celeste agreed to the production of a Christmas medley recording using electronically reproduced and arranged calls that Freddy would coach from the bird. They also agreed to a line of "feather art," and spent an hour over a hot copying machine, pressing the bird's open wings, its sides, and sometimes the back of its head to the photostatic surface. These images were later faxed to agents in L. A. and New York.

When their business in the city was finished, they loaded the truck with the many things they'd bought at the malls and the warehouse stores, and they began the drive home to the cousin's cabin. It was evening by the time they left, and so it was fullest dark when they reached the pass and stopped at the lonely restroom there, lit by a single floodlight over the doorway.

Celeste was a long time in the restroom, and while she was, Freddy shoved around their new luggage full of new clothes, Celeste's new sunlamp, his new Swedish chainsaw, all the components for a first-class home entertainment center, and the largest imaginable box of tortilla chips, until he could reach the kennel. He opened the wire gate and took out the bird, and he set the bird in a snowfield on the far side of the road. He climbed up on a snow berm behind the building, away from the circle of light, and just stood there with his hands in his pockets and his head all the way back, looking straight up at the sky. There were no clouds, no moon, only stars by the zillions, as thick as spruce pollen in the spring.

"Criminy!" Celeste humped out of the restroom. "I about froze my tail off."

"Come up here," Freddy said.

Celeste had to look to find him on the berm. "What the dingdang are you doing up there?"

Freddy held out his hand.

She made her way over the walk and around the hard lumps of old plowed snow, and then she reached up and took his hand and was hauled up the berm. "What?" she said, panting huge vaporous clouds that froze like confectioner's sugar to her frazzles of hair.

"The stars."

Celeste locked her arm around Freddy's waist, and they both looked at the zillions of stars in the clear, clear sky until Celeste grew dizzy, and if Freddy hadn't steadied her, she might have pitched sideways off the berm.

"That story," Freddy said. "When Raven went up the smoke hole? It was because he was creating the heavens. Before that, there wasn't any light in the world. It was dark all the time. An old man had the stars, the moon, and the sun in boxes in his house. Raven let the stars out of a box, and they flew up through the smoke hole and filled the heavens. Then he let the moon out, and it went through the smoke hole. Then he took the sun, and he pushed it in front of him through that smoke hole and carried it all the way up and hung it in the sky. That's how he got black, going through the smoke hole with the sun."

Celeste pulled Freddy closer. "You don't really believe that."

Freddy looked at the stars and they burned a little brighter, and all over the rolling treeless landscape, particles of snow picked up the starlight, sparking and flaring. He said, "It doesn't matter if anyone believes it. The stars are there just the same. And the moon and sun. And, you know, Raven was also a trickster."

Just then a huge white bird with darting eyes rose from across the way and flew straight up toward the stars. It was magnificent again, whitest of white, with long shapely wing feathers and sculptured shoulders. The bird's jubilant beak was thrown wide open, and its tongue flapped out like a whip end. The feet were tucked in tight against the perfect belly down, the rings on the toes just barely visible, winking light. Freddy watched the bird go, watched it wheel and spiral and somersault as it ascended, but he didn't point it out to Celeste, who just at the same moment was looking instead at the steady lights of a late jet plane, heading south and full of sleeping people.

Afterlife

IT'S ALL CRAP, he tells himself, all through the night and into the next morning, as he throws covers off and, shivering, piles them back on, as he stands heaving over the toilet bowl, as the maids knock around in the hall, bumping their brooms into corners and barking a language that's all hisses and throaty coughs. He's only sick, poisoned most likely by meatballs or mayonnaise at that diner, where the music was too thumpy and a little kid, with a mouth like a perfect round "o", had been coughing all over the counter. Maybe he was already sick before then, a hotdog back at the border, or some of that deep-fat grease they use over and over; maybe he had already started the fever that made everything, all of it, seem too much.

He can't stand to think of food, and these are the very images—those meatballs in gravy, the greasy doughnut with watery coffee—that keep sneaking into the corners of his mind to trip new waves of nausea. Although whatever he ate has long been expelled from both ends, still his stomach twists inside out as he hugs the toilet, spitting yellow bile, and his butt squirts and must be tortured again with the cheap, rough-as-newsprint toilet paper.

In a cooler moment, as he lies in his shit-smelling bed, he tells himself once more that there is no relationship. Whatever happened in Alaska has nothing to do with his being sick. He didn't spend a lifetime in sales and not learn that you get away with what you get away with, and the meek certainly do not inherit anything but grief. Anything else is superstition, which is the same as ignorance.

Kevin Schmidt is neither superstitious nor ignorant. He's sick, through no fault of his own except for maybe being too reckless in his selection of dining facilities. Not that there are a great number of five-star restaurants along the Alaska-Canada highway, or that his summer's work left him with a five-star bankroll. He lies with clenched buttocks and tries to think of happier things—San Diego sun, the smell of new cars, his own backyard swimming pool. Soon, when she's back from visiting her sister, he'll call his wife. Soon he'll be well, he'll be back on the road, he'll be home.

Ⓢ

When the fever returns like a hot fog that swirls past the insides of his eyeballs, he experiences something that is either a bad, waking dream or a hallucination. In it, he sees himself following a creek that winds into the distance, and then there's a passageway beneath it, so that he's looking up from below, seeing the water wash past in ripples and the blue sky beyond, like looking through the glass bottom of a boat, only upside down, and the place he's in is more tunnel-like, dry and cavernous. He knows where he's going, and he doesn't want to go there, but the tunnel is closing behind him, zipping like a ziploc bag, so that there's nothing for him but to continue up the creek, under the creek. He hears water rumbling overhead and then, through it, the beginnings of the cries, and then he comes upon the first bodies, which are insect parts—disconnected legs, flaky wings, a fly's multi-faceted eye. They lie on the hard cement of the tunnel and quiver. Fish parts come next, great piles of heads, and then birds—gulls—bloody and torn, with broken feathers and shattered bones. The sounds they make are like air sucking

NANCY LORD

through chest wounds—pitiful exhausted wheezes, squeaks. They wave crooked and scaly toes.

He is, he knows, in the place where dead animals go to be reborn. How he knows this he doesn't know, and even as he knows it, he also knows that he is in a motel room where someone's flushed toilet is sending water through the pipes within his wall, and that he read something like this, about places for dead animals, once. He reads a lot, and most of what he reads is adventure stories and Indian stuff, and some of this Indian stuff has stuck in his brain. The tunnel, now, has got him surrounded, and the ziploc is squeezing him from behind. He must continue forward. He *must*, because he is implicated here. He is, he understands, not only responsible for deaths—the insects he swatted, the fish he caught, the birds he pot-shot; the dead animals piled here are in agony and are not recycling through into newborn animals because he did it all wrong.

Wrong, wrong, wrong pounds through his head like a big iron plate being whacked by a mallet.

A seal, oozing oil and putrification, blocks his path. He hadn't meant to kill it; in fact, until this moment, he didn't know he had. He'd just shot at it, because it was there, and because it ate salmon and he wanted to catch more salmon. It had been a long way off, just a bob of a head, and he hadn't meant to even hit it.

After that, the carnage gets worse. It's not all *his* carnage, but it all stinks and cries out and twitches, and it's divided into body parts that are missing other body parts and so form great heaps of dismembered, tortured-looking rot, with plucked eyes and bursting guts.

Murmuring, like a low voice in his ear, seeps through the tunnel wall. The words are unrecognizable but the thought is whole and clear. *These are the animals that cannot return to life because they were so mistreated.*

He feels weak, as though his legs may collapse under him, and then he wakes in his motel bed with light slipping through the opening that will not close between the two sections of plastic curtain, and he is almost glad to remember where he is and how sick he's been and to feel sorry for himself. Dreams are—well, just dreams—and there's no such thing as reincarnation, but still, he lies there and thinks about that place under a creek and why he feels guilty and grateful all at the same time. Guilty because, yes, he did kill animals, and not always in a hunting situation, and grateful—well, because he woke up. He knew in the dream—if that's what it was—that there was more around the next bloody corner, and he didn't want to go there.

~

When he thinks about him, he gets mad at the old fisherman. He, Kevin Schmidt, had only wanted a summer in Alaska, some fishing, looking around, a chance at his piece of the last frontier before it was all gone. He was happy enough living in his camper and working at that cannery, even if he was more than twice the age of all those goofy college kids. Then the old man showed up and offered him a fishing job. Sounded good, right? Not so good. There were hardly any salmon to catch, but there was instead a heck of a lot of free work he was supposed to do for the old man, and he had to share a cabin—more like a shack—with a Bible-quoting drunk. Just the two of them stuck in that plywood shack, and every day they had to hike to the old man's palatial-by-comparison camp to cut firewood and wrestle logs out of a creek and a couple of times a week go out in a tippy boat to tie nets in the water and not catch any fish. On top of that, the drunk brought not his share of food from town but only cheap whiskey and then passed out on the beach and had to be carried in and put to bed. He was useless and he, Kevin Schmidt, had to do the work for both of them, even though they got paid the same crew share, which was ten percent of nothing.

For all that, he deserved *something*.

Each time the fever comes, certain words get into his head and keep pounding, as though there's something about them he needs to memorize. This time, he falls into a litany of numbers, of weapons, gauges, the guns he'd taken to Alaska, which are now sealed as required by Canadian law, untouchable until he's back in the good old U.S.A. *Thirty-ought-six*, he keeps hearing, the numbers spelled out like words, the zero with that tight sound of obligation. *Thirty-eight. Twenty-two. Shotgun. Shot gun*, those two short vowels that might as well be numbers. He owns them all, and more. He knows how to use them. He's an outdoorsman. *Out doors man.*

On the beach, right in front of his cabin, those bears had paced back and forth, rolling their shoulders like wrestlers, chomping their jaws. The world's largest carnivores, they were; they could rip a person in two with one swat of a meat-hook paw. He wasn't sure who was doing the stalking—he of them, or they of him. Definitely they were unafraid. Definitely he crept up on them, along the path and through the grass; he positioned himself carefully. If he missed . . . Bears could run as fast as horses. He knew all this; he had read the books—*Bear Tales* and *More Bear Tales*. He took careful aim. He squeezed. He nailed the one. The other kept coming. He squeezed again and watched it fall. Man against beast, and he had triumphed. It wasn't everywhere you could shoot a brown bear anymore, but he had come to Alaska and done it.

He is entirely rational now—almost light-headed. He is aware of the daylight suffusing his gray room and the wind that rattles the window, which is otherwise sealed shut. Overhead, the light fixture is a flattish, squarish piece of glass over a single bulb; he notices both that it is not squared to the shape of the room, and that dead flies on the bulb side are visible through the milky glass, scattered like raisins in bread. He can, without any trouble at all, remember why he likes to hunt, the feeling he gets pitting his skill against an animal's strength and evasiveness. *Taking* the animal. *His* deer, antelope, quail, and the odd wily coyote. He would love to go up north and hunt a polar bear. Or to Africa for lions. Or find himself staring down a Siberian tiger. He would possess them all.

With the brown bears, admittedly, it was not entirely a matter of hunting. It was, as much as anything, self-protection. He didn't like having to look behind himself every time he stepped out to take a whizz.

Alaska was, moreover, full of bears. Alaska practically manufactured bears, and he didn't know why there wasn't a wide-open season on them, even a bounty where they were hazardous to people. It was a rip-off, really, what they charged for a license if you didn't live there, and then there were certain limited areas and seasons, none of which were convenient, and usually you had to hire a guide. It was just another way of getting money from non-Alaskans, except he wasn't having any of it. He still lived in a free country, and he would protect his own backside.

He feels the pressure coming again and barely makes it into the bathroom. The exploding sounds are disgustingly loud, grotesque. He's lucky, he supposes, to be in a place where no one knows him from Moses, though on the other hand he would dearly love sympathy and a cool wet rag held to his brow. Whenever he's sick he thinks not of his wife, who's usually working, but of his mother, who, when he was a boy, brought him glasses of ginger ale and new toy soldiers that smelled of warm plastic and begged to be chewed.

He sits on the toilet for a long time. He rests with his hot head on his crossed arms on his hairy thighs while he squeezes and waits and wonders if he could die from food poisoning and, if he did, how long it would be before the maids or the management would disregard the DO NOT DISTURB hanger on his door and look in. He hates it when he reads things in the newspaper that say that someone detected a bad odor, and then the door was opened, and some poor bastard had been dead for days or weeks.

With his head down, he sees those bears again, only this time he knows they're not so huge or fierce or threatening. They're playing on the beach, bumping one another, pouncing, dashing around boulders. One wades into the water and stands on a rock, then climbs down and mouths something—seaweed?—from its side. They're the size of large dogs—yearling bears, siblings, one blond and one brown, and they have been around, off and on, for weeks. The woman who lives down the beach in the opposite direction from the old fisherman has told him how much she likes watching them. She has also lectured him about keeping "a clean camp" so as not to tempt the bears with food. Foolish woman, she doesn't even own a gun, and once she asked him, when she saw him shooting seagulls, what he was doing. He had not let her get to him.

Those yearling bears should have been with a sow, but they weren't; somehow they had lost their mother. Without her, they didn't know wariness, didn't know they needed to keep away from people. He went out from his cabin and watched them. They saw him and went on playing. He walked right up close and shot one and then the other. They were as easy as paper targets.

Back in bed, he tells himself that they were—really—dangerous, precisely because they weren't afraid. And without a mother, they wouldn't learn what they needed to learn. They wouldn't eat enough. Other bears would kill them. Other people would shoot them. One way or another, they wouldn't survive the summer, or the fall, or the long winter.

After a while he sleeps again, and it's not so fevered but a sleep of exhaustion, as though every bit of him is wrung out. It becomes evening and night, and a siren wails, and then people check in to the room behind his headboard, and the sounds of them climbing on and off one another, moaning and crying out and sucking, and the sticky slaps of damp skin all get mixed up in his mind with those two bears.

Because, in fact, they were not exactly like paper targets. And they did not fall down quite so neatly and quietly.

The dark one, the one he shot first, spun around as though it thought it was stung by a bee, with a little yelp, and then it caved onto the sand, hard on its side.

The blond one was a little farther off, and it didn't run away, as he thought it might, and should. Instead, it came back to the brown one and stared at it, and walked around it. He shot at it, and it just stood there and looked puzzled, and then its legs folded and it went down. It was not dead, and it did not die, but its back legs were helpless, paralyzed. Its front legs pulled it around in circles. And it cried—screeched really, a pitiful savage kind of sound, while it spun like a top, clawing the sand, sending sand up in sprays all around.

He shot it in the head after that. He remembers now he'd been surprised, the way the eyes had teared into the long grooves that went down the sides of the snout, and the snout was strung with ropes of saliva, like noodles. It had wet and shit all over itself and was not very dignified in its death.

He saw it was a female, and the other one a male, and then he went inside and got his knife.

On the other side of the wall, now, the bed has stopped bumping and someone is crying, not loudly but in a way that suggests to him either very great happiness or deep regret, possibly both.

He sleeps again, in the crying and the murmuring and his own exhaustion, and even before he loses consciousness, he knows he will be back in the tunnel, under the water, in the place where animals go to be reborn, in the hellish part of it where they might wait an eternity. He knows it, and when he finds himself there, within the tunnel and the inside of his skull, he sees the twin mounds of skinned bears. The flesh is sun-baked, stuck with sand, swollen, writhing with maggots. One corpse is turned on its back, one on its belly. Heads are twisted; legs are spread. They look violated in every way. Tufts of fur blow past his feet, and the stench overcomes him.

He barely makes it to the toilet, where, when he's done retching, he rests his head against the cool tank. The room, with its sealed window, stinks. He takes all his soiled clothes from the floor and puts them into a plastic garbage bag, which he ties tight at the top. He gets back into bed, and the bed stinks. He turns his pillow over, and the room, the covers, the air still smell like shit. He showers and gets back into bed, and the smell is still so bad it will not let him sleep. He thinks it will suffocate him. He wonders if he should ask the maids to change his bed, but he's too embarrassed. He wonders if he got shit on the rug during one of his runs to the toilet.

He wonders if the tides are rising or falling now, whether the water is closer to or farther from the two skinned-out bears left like that, on the beach. He and the drunk had salted the two skins, packed them up, departed the next day, stiffing the old fisherman for the rest of the so-called fishing season, but too bad, because the way he figured it, he was losing money every day he stayed. Not that money was a big thing for Kevin Schmidt. He had enough he could buy that old fisherman ten times over. No, money wasn't it. But he didn't like being treated like a Mexican.

He went to Alaska, and, for his trouble, he has his bear skin.

When he finally thinks he will neither vomit nor shit his pants, he gets dressed and, very shaky still, ventures out to buy a 7-UP from a machine, then continues out to breathe pure Canadian air and to make sure his rig is still parked in the lot. For a while he stands and breathes and sways in the wind, taking small sips from his soda and looking at a display of license plates from all over the States and Canada. His clothes feel loose, like he's lost a lot of weight, like he's frail, and old, like he's a leaf that might blow across the road. He will have to eat, but not yet. His stomach growls; he was thirsty, and the soda felt good in his throat, but his stomach resists.

When he opens the back of his camper, it takes all his energy to dig around and under to pull out his bedroll. He had wrapped the salted skin inside it, inside plastic, to hide it from the customs agents. Without a tag, they would have jumped all over him. But he never has any trouble, anywhere, getting searched, because he knows how to talk to people. Hey, he hadn't made a fortune in sales by looking like a suspicious character.

There, in the dirt parking lot, with the early-August, end-of-summer traffic rocketing past, Kevin Schmidt unrolls his bedroll and looks at the bear skin therein. He peels away the plastic to expose the matted blond fur that looks—well, flat, and not nearly as thick or golden as he'd remembered. And the entire skin—it's not very long or wide, not large at all. He sinks his hands into the fur, squeezing fistfuls, possessing it, wanting the beauty of that bear and its strength and yes, its innocence. He tries to see the skin, cleaned and cured and glued to felt, in his home, among all the rest that he has so well earned, but the fever must still be upon him, because he still smells stink, and he knows in a way that is illogical that those bloated, abused, and unforgiving bodies are still waiting and will wait for him while he vomits onto his shoes.

Trip Report (Confidential)

MOJACAR, SPAIN

ACCESS:

Wretched bus trip—9 hours through crumbling rock country and squalid villages (no facilities on bus, but three stops), surly drivers, no English, no familiarity with visitor industry. Absolutely we'll need a modern on-site airport, direct connections, charters. Possible also to have cruise ships (casino?) arrive by water. (Need dock or lightering facilities—check water depths.) My butt's still vibrating from the long, dusty road, and the woman who sat next to me on the return, though she left her farm animals at home, smelled like a goat.

IMPRESSIONS:

Village itself highly scenic, think Cinderella castle plus Frontierland and the Tree-of-Life nighttime glow, a touch of Taos, maybe even Malibu potential (well maybe not, but there *is* a coastline and water just down the road). Photos accurate (see more I took plus postcards). Whitewashed buildings on hill (Moorish, as in *mosqueteer?*), crammed together, narrow streets, flowers, people generally friendly. Certain amount of more crumbling buildings and trash, cats with runny eyes, several centuries of piss-smell—nothing our reclamation people and a few exterminators can't fix. Steep, heart-thumping climb through village. Scenic view of Mediterranean, dry rocky (crumbling) hills, dry river valley, orange and lemon groves.

Presently minor resort town—Spanish in summer, a few Nordic types in winter. Comfortable winter temperatures, hot in summer (no more so than Orlando). Sun 340+ days per year. Real estate dazzlingly cheap. Purchase of whole town within possibility. See file re: property values, sample establishments. (I was very discrete in all inquiries, just another *fureigner* looking for escape.)

Real authenticity: Tiny old women in black, great wrinkled faces, cute as a pack of Minnie Mouses. Guy with some goats. (Goat shit a problem—all over roads—and low-slung swollen udders unsightly. Keep in restricted area, possible petting zoo depending on Animal Kingdom reviews.) Sense of being frozen in time, some ancient past. Possible local employment for "color," female cast members dress as in old (scarves over heads, water jugs on heads). People generally good-looking but could use a little help with hygiene in the deodorant categories. Way more agreeable than the French.

CONCEPT:

As discussed previously, combination of theme park (fun), Graceland (nostalgia), Sturbridge Village (quaint history, culture), and Club Med (nude beaches?, at least separate adults and families, as at Bahamas site). Target audience—well-heeled internationals but particularly Americans, boomer generation, family, grandchildren, singles/divorced looking. Market at Eurodisney as sidetrip for more adventurous. Segmented developments to appeal to all. Key words: celebrate the heritage, create new memories, magical adventures, traditionally inspired, classics.

Names—Mojacar Disney, Disney Start, First Disney,

Disney Home, Disney Inspiration, Old World Disney, Disney Magic. (My vote Old World Disney — Mojacar). Nickname Mo' Disney?

As we all remember, previous attempt (1940) to obtain birth certificate was unsuccessful (turned into toilet paper during Spanish war). But, oral history/local knowledge informed and adamant—only the variations are variable. In addition to what we have from the Archives and the Mosley book (Consuela Suarez version), here's what I discretely picked up from enthusiastic (and utterly convinced and convincing) locals:

VERSION #1. Seems to be the more official one—heard from assistant to the mayor. Walt born in 1901 as José Guiraro, to a (apparently unmarried—also exceptionally beautiful) laundress named Isabel Zamora. The mother immediately emigrated to Chicago, where she had a brother, and, once there, gave up the child to adoption by a family named Disney. (Hence the long insistence that Walt was born in Chicago and 100% true-blood American.)

VERSION #2. Definitely more colorful (and less likely) of the two, from old woman who runs a hostal, translated by a young girl. Walt's father worked at the docks in a nearby coastal village, where the captain of a ship from Boston that visited regularly noticed the boy and took him on several journeys (cabin boy, I think). Father died when Walt was 12, and mother asked ship captain to take both of them to America. He did, and they (mother and son) ended up working on a farm in California. Mother died, and owner of farm, named Walter Disney, adopted the boy.

A slight variation of this, heard from local man in cantina, in poor but understandable English, has 12-year-old Walt running away from his impoverished, boring, possibly abusive (goat-stinky?) family, as a stowaway on a ship to the Canary Islands and then to America, where he took an American name and, through hard work and good luck, became the magnificent success that he was, beloved by all, blah blah, the cantina guy was a major fan. He moreover swore that his father remembered the young Walt, a tall skinny kid with a pinched face.

Negatives (certainly nothing fatal). Both versions fit romantic rags-to-riches theme, but both have possible "ethnic problem." Walt as José? (Reminds one of bad Mexican jokes.) Maybe translate to Joseph? Also, Guiraro not a name Americans can get their tongues around, and just not very appealing (sounds like a lizard?) Version 1 also has the problems of illegitimacy and short residency (but Zamora a nice-sounding name).

Overall, good material. Tragic death of father—drowning at dock? lost at sea? crushed by fallen rock walls? (note: rock walls everywhere here—very scenic, possibly need reinforcement for safety.) Beautiful laundress mother (more about her place of work and other family landmarks later).

Focus group issues of ethnicity and illegitimacy. (With Hispanic pop. so high and multiculturalism so hot, not surprised if we run up some significant positives.) Post-Clinton, etc., no shame to honest origins.

SPECIAL OPPORTUNITIES:
The usual unsurpassed fun, of course. Check with development and marketing people. Exhibits, rides, shops, restaurants, etc.

Fountain. Special feature is this ancient spot in village

where spring water comes out of mountain, where people even today come for drinking water and to wash clothes. Where Walt drank, where his mother did laundry business. Sell bottles and jugs of water. (Ceramic jugs also very attractive, sellable.) Possible water rides? Reenactments of lovely Isabel scrubbing the dirt out of little Walt's diapers?

Capitalize on local oranges, lemons, almonds, as well as water. Drinks, etc. Spanish food (not too ethnic), overpriced tapas.

Zamora house. Was lucky to find this. Nice whitewashed house in valley below village, with stable, old olive oil mill, now belonging to farmer. Previously purchased from Zamora family, which otherwise seems to have disappeared. No idea if Isabel's (and Walt's) family, but good enough. Humble home without being squalid. Plenty of space around for parking, additional development (air-conditioned theaters for films, live stage performances?).

Centennial of birth. 2001. Can we make it? Talk to planners.

Interactive museum. Lots of Disney facts, artifacts, memorabilia. Computer quizzes, big screens, buttons to push, all that screaming-kid stuff. Story of birth, early life. Story of animation, blah blah.

Med. Beaches close by. Summers hot. Water slides, wave pools, pirate ships, swan boats? Reconstructed Boston ship that took Walt to America? Etc. Reemphasized or new characters, movie and toy, merchandise tie-ins. Figure out (archivists, creative people) which characters, landscapes, cartoons could have some remote connection to this place, for remarketing. Aladdin, desert stuff—sand, cactus, swaybacked donkeys, cats, goats. Anything with pirates and mermaids, ships. Women in robes with water jugs on heads? Cinderella, washing all those clothes. Zorro. Possible new movie with Spanish theme? Cabin boy something-or-other?

Moving sidewalk tour through scenic village streets. Animated figures?

Golf. Darn good course exists. Only need to purchase and themize.

NECESSARY INFRASTRUCTURE:

Airport, as mentioned, and ground transportation (monorail? moving sidewalks? some kind of step-on, step-off delivery system). Whatever it takes for steep grades (no heart attacks) and handicap access (ADA standards?).

Possible desalination plant. Water scarce. (Check engineers.)

Own generation. Local is unreliable and most likely insufficient. Solar power? No air-conditioning in use at present. (Engineers: figure BTUs for heating and cooling.)

Hotels, etc. Lots of cheap land in valley below, cheap workforce. (Maintain "mosqueteer" theme, add sparkly stucco, wet bars.)

COMPETITION:

None. Although story seems well known, no one has opportunized. I searched shops and found a single Mickey Mouse T-shirt (purchased to test whether shopkeeper would tell me something about Walt, which she did not.) Could be our earlier efforts to quash any claims in this direction (e.g., insisting on removal of "birthplace" sign) were thoroughly successful.

Town does have a symbol known as the indalo, which comes from some ancient figure and is all over the current crop of key chains and coffee mugs. Hideous figure of man with arms and legs extended and what appears to be a rather long penis. (Lawyers: create as trademark, then forbid other use?)

SUMMARY/RECS:

All earlier info confirms. Untapped wealth, chance to make up for Eurodisaster and tap trends (nostalgia, millennial, multicult). Recommend development team meet ASAP. Walt would be proud (?).

Candace Counts Coup

I N A CROWD, you would notice Candace. She wore a large
gold nose ring. Her hair, in front and on top, was purple.
Neither the nose ring nor the purple hair would be remarkable
on a teenager, but you would notice them on a fifty-five-year-old
head that was otherwise unadorned and capped by gray, largely
straight and somewhat thinning hair. Because Candace's face
tended to be very large and her eyes very small, she somewhat
resembled a buffalo. The nose ring was something she had chosen, perhaps for effect. The purple hair had just happened.
Somehow, painting, purple paint had come to be all through the
bangs and crown of Candace's hair, and there it stayed.

As it stayed on her clothes, which tended to be shifts made
from enormous expanses of fabric. Some were tie-dyed. Some
just looked that way. Some were fluorescent. In all of them,
Candace's massive, generally unrestricted breasts bulged at the
front, the fat at her waist stretched the seams so that the stitches
and the space between stitches showed, her meaty knees and
long-haired calves protruded. When she walked, her thighs
rubbed with a sound like pieces of vinyl mating. Her feet
scuffed on the floor, on the broken pavement, *shh–shh–shh*, her
sandals taking little tiny, crepe-soled steps.

She would never think of herself as brave. She was just
Candace. It was the rest of us who came to call her Brave Woman.

Candace was an artist. Not an ordinary artist, not what you
think. She didn't do sketches or paintings or etchings, not carv-
ings or ceramics or quilts. She didn't do the kinds of things that

could go into a gallery, or on an art lover's wall. Her art wasn't the kind anyone, no matter how avant-garde or unreasonably rich and hip or poor in taste, would, or could, *buy*.

Candace called herself an installation artist, which meant that her pieces were constructed to go into particular venues. They were conceived as parts of places and assembled for those places, and when the time was up, they were removed from those places, usually, for lack of space in Candace's life, to the dump. They were, by their nature, ephemeral. It was hard to get even the government to pay for something here today and gone tomorrow.

For example, one of Candace's recent uncommissioned installations was for an outdoor pavilion. She had sewn a wonderful parachute-like thing out of, well, parachutes and road fabric, and painted it to look like flames. Hanging there from the roof, it had billowed in the wind, looking in fact very much like flickering fire. She'd outfitted the entire student body of the neighboring grade school to look like little brown roasting nuts, and placed them under the pavilion, and she had sat in the center, dressed as a marshmallow. People—mostly the parents of the students, who thought what-the-heck-now—showed up to look at her installation, and then, because the hanging-down fabric truly was a fire hazard, or so the fire marshall said, the whole work of art, minus its human component, was torn down and trucked off to the dump, where some said the parachute and road fabric materials were meant to go to directly, or perhaps had come from.

Candace's commitment to her nonrenumerative art meant that, among artists, she was the poorest of the poor.

But still, somehow she found rent money, food, materials

NANCY LORD

for her work. It helped that her father was still living and that he, despite being a capitalist enslaver, had always had a fondness for his daughter, if not for her art. Maybe it was guilt he felt. Who knows?

⌒

That morning, when Candace awoke in her low-rent basement apartment, it was to the screams of a woman overhead and a sound like *clunk-a-clunk-a-clunk,* someone smashing that woman's head against the bare floor. The noise had entered Candace's dreams as buzzards screeching over a nearly dead African animal of some hoof-stomping kind, but as soon as she was awake, she lost no time in wrapping herself in a large paint-covered sheet and running—well, rushing, faster than you might think—up the flight of stairs, where she pounded on the paneled door and then, using a stepladder someone had left in the hall, broke through the door.

It was hard for her to both hold onto her sheet and to do something about the man who was holding a weeping woman by the hair, so when she let go of the sheet, the man was so stunned that he instantly put his hands up in front of him. Candace nonetheless pushed him back and then sat on him, while the woman, clutching her bruised neck, crawled away.

"Call 9-1-1," Candace said. The woman hesitated a moment and then, as though she found Candace too frightening to not obey, did as she was told.

The man underneath Candace bellowed and twisted and swore. "Please," he begged. "They'll put me in jail. What is this shit? I don't deserve this! Please! Get off me! I can't breathe!"

Candace did not know either of her upstairs neighbors

from Adam and Eve, though she thought she might have seen the woman a time or two going in and out of the building. She said, "You think I like this? You woke me up, *and* I haven't even had time to wash the sleep out of my eyes. I've had zero cups of coffee and my mouth tastes like snakebite. I've got no clothes. You think I want to have to explain this situation to pistol-packing, flagrantly abusive peace officers at this hour of the pre-dawn morning? I don't even know what time it is. What time is it?"

The man wouldn't tell her and the woman didn't seem to know. There was no clock in the room that Candace could see, though she did see the big-screen TV, the metal legs of a kitchen table, a painting on the wall of cats with a ball of yarn. These people had no taste at all. She began to sing something she'd heard on the radio the night before, an old sad Billie Holiday song about bad luck and trouble. She didn't have much of a voice, but the song, you could say, was called for under the circumstances.

"Cut the crap!" the man shouted.

Candace shifted her weight and heard something crack. Something in the floor, maybe, something in the man's pocket, something in the man. He groaned, and she thought, *maybe a rib*. She placed her marsupial feet firmly over the man's wrists and said to the woman, "Could you please hand me my cape?" As best she could, she wrapped herself up again. She thought but did not say, *so shall ye reap,* and she meant both the man and the woman. She suspected they deserved one another, though nobody deserved to get their head smashed on the floor. She thought she herself deserved to reap a little more artistic recognition, but she was not complaining. She did not look for earthly rewards.

Later, there was a little trouble about the man's medical bills, the broken door, rudeness to officers who also apparently had not had their morning coffee, and Candace's removal of the offending painting. Candace was informed that it was very dangerous to involve herself in domestic violence situations and that next time she should call the police and wait for them to handle the situation professionally. To which she said, "Right. Like I'm going to listen to someone get killed." That morning, she had only done what anyone in her position would do. Or should do. She did not consider herself heroic, only human.

That morning, still before seven A.M., Candace returned to her apartment, where she washed, dressed, drank coffee, blew the insides out of six dozen white-shelled eggs she needed for her work, ate two eggs scrambled, and put five dozen and ten eggs down the toilet because the neighborhood soup kitchen would not accept eggs outside of their shells and would not blow eggs themselves, even if she donated them. She ate toast with jam and experimented on white bread slices with a blowtorch to create pieces that, together, formed a mosaic portrait of someone looking very much like Richard Nixon in his better days.

On her way to her installation site in a warehouse just a few blocks away, *shh-shh-shhing* in her sandals over the paving stones, the grates, the dirt and broken glass, she stopped numerous times with her box of blown egg shells packed in popcorn. The box was not heavy, only awkward. As she rested it on steps, railings, the bumpers of cars, she studied the life around her. A hawkish bird soared overhead. Someone shouted in a language she didn't know, something that sounded like *car-luffle-lay*. A delivery truck with squeaky brakes rolled past her. She examined a stained, cushionless settee poised at the curb and left it, regretfully, though she thought she might come back with her little chainsaw and take the hardwood legs. She glanced into the shopping cart of a raggedy man going through a dumpster.

"You got any polka dots or pantyhose?" she asked the man. "I'm looking for anything polka-dotted, and any color pantyhose or stockings but especially fishnet. And sneakers, especially the old cloth or canvas kind." She had an idea, just that morning, for a few hundred painted sneakers on a wire, all dancing in the wind. Or the wire could be connected to a motor that gave it a good, constant jiggle, and she wouldn't need wind.

The man shook his head and tossed two aluminum cans into the cart. "Sorry. But if you got some change you could spare, I could get something to eat and not get another bellyache from the spoiled cakes."

Candace set down her box and unzipped the leather purse she wore belted around her middle. She handed the man a crumpled dollar bill and some change. She knew she wasn't supposed to. Everyone said to give to charities instead, if you wanted to help, but to her it made sense to give directly to people who needed it. She would want them—anyone—to do the same for her. What was the point of money, anyway? This was a discussion she had had many times with her father and many other accumulative people.

"God bless you," the man said.

What social agency ever thanked her like that? What institutional face looked as grateful as that one, cavernous and yellow-eyed as it might necessarily be?

Candace walked another half-block, looking at the facades of buildings, their faded inscriptions and gargoyles, and thinking what she could do with them with a little dynamite and reassembly, a little wire and paint. She was dreaming this—building walls of Roman numerals and angels with facial hair and pink private parts—when a car, an old blue Mercury, ran up on the sidewalk and into the iron gate across a liquor store doorway, missing Candace by ten feet. It was an easy calculation for Candace to see that if she had not been asked for change by the man in the dumpster and had not fished around in her waist purse for precisely the minute that she had, she would have found herself square in the car's path.

Candace set her box down again. The car had not been going fast, and she had watched the people's heads, when the car came to its abrupt stop, fling forward and back, together. She had seen the bigness of their eyes and the way their arms thrust out in front of them. It was a dramatic moment that impressed her, even without inflating airbags, with its artistic potential. What luck besides! The car, going over the curb, had kicked off a hubcap, which now spun in the street like a wavering, unbalanced top, and the muffler. Candace helped the two stunned people—an older, church-dressed couple—from the car, and after ascertaining their physical well-being, she asked if she might have the hubcap and the muffler, which they said she could. She went off again with her box of egg shells topped with the warm muffler set inside the hubcap like a leg of lamb on a platter. It was amazing to her, always, that the very things she needed had a way of appearing in her path as agreeably as that.

When Candace reached the warehouse, she only dropped off her materials and took a look at the shape of what she had so far: a collection of shiny metallic car parts, egg shells (some of them glued to painted cardboard), pairs of pantyhose stretched from ceiling to floor and anchored with bricks, paving stones, and blocks of crumbled cement, which she'd fed down the legs and into the toes (causing numerous runs), the polka-dotted clothing she had yet to tear into strips and integrate into the background. The piece had to do with chaos theory, the way molecules organized themselves, and technology as organized chaos; it was still coming to her—the patterns of randomness, the beauty of repetitions and waves, the way things would finally fit together within her artistic vision.

She had more to think about, so she took the subway across town to the botanical garden, where she wandered through the misty humidity and various exotic ecosystems, searching for lilies, carnivorous flycatchers, cacti, the baby sequoia trees. She went around leaning over the rails to sniff one flower and another. She wanted an olfactory element to her work, and she had to meditate on what to include, what effect she would get from apple blossom, tiger lily, the tropical hibiscus. She let her nose draw her around the walkways, *shuffle-shuffle-sniff.* She closed her eyes. The scents were like colors, not the colors of blossoms, but something more—more peaches, more pastels, more and deeper blues and purples. She let her nose sort out the differences, the singular shades and strands; she thought how she would paint the dots of scents, the waves of stripey smells, how she could get the essences into sprays that were not stinky perfumes or piney room fresheners, but themselves, one scent and sense blending to another.

She was thinking these things, and about taste, too, and why the smell and taste of some things, like vanilla, were not quite the same. When she reached the prickly pear cactus and found it in full, luscious red fruit, she reached across the rail and broke off a piece. It tasted good, like honeyed water, like a juicier plum. It was not until she was leaving that a woman in charge looked at her strangely and said, "What's that on your face? Are you bleeding?" and she wiped away a part of the cactus fruit that had stuck there.

"Just cactus fruit," she said.

The woman looked at her with even more concern. *"Our* cactus fruit? You weren't eating from the plants in the green-house, were you?"

Candace knew the correct answer would be *no*. But, like little George Washington and unlike another president she could name, she could not tell a lie. "Just a taste," she said. "I never tasted one before."

The woman looked as stern as a nun, and like she'd use a ruler on Candace's knuckles, if she had one. "The plants here belong to *everyone*. They're not for any one person's personal use. Plus," she said, "we are not liable for poisoning. Many of our plants are extremely toxic."

But Candace knew that plants liked to be eaten. There was an old Indian belief she'd learned from an old Indian boyfriend, that plants gave themselves for people to use, and if you didn't use them, didn't eat them and make your baskets from them, they would quit offering themselves. Which was maybe one of the principal problems in the modern world and why we were stuck with iceberg lettuce.

Candace put her hand on the woman's wrist. At first she

felt the woman draw back, but then she felt the transfer of energy between them. The cactus fruit had entered her, was at that moment being transformed into a part of her, and the molecules were tripping right through her, down her arm, across her fingertips, to a person who needed to lighten up and who now, surely, in Candace's cosmogonic belief, would.

Outside the botanical garden, Candace immediately came upon a man walking a very thin, dispirited-looking spaniel-style dog.

"Your dog is way too thin," Candace said to him. "You're either starving the poor animal or it has worms."

"Thank you for your expert opinion," the man said.

Candace stooped beside the dog and rubbed its head and bony back. The dog wagged its tail. "Yes, you're a nice doggy," she said, "and your master is a sorry piece of shit."

"I should kick your fat ass across the street," the man said.

Candace stood up. She was a little taller than the man and outweighed him by at least one hundred pounds. She tapped him on the chest, on the front of his alligator shirt. "Just try it," she said. She blew from her bottom lip, so that the gray and mostly purple hair hanging over her eyes fluttered. She stared down the man, who seemed to withdraw behind the surprise, then the fear, in his eyes, until his face was a blank. "So take this dog home and make him a doctor's appointment, or the next time I see you, you will become horsemeat yourself. *Do you understand?*" She pressed her finger into his chest and felt him lean away.

"I'm not looking for any trouble," the man said.

"Good. I'm sure you love your dog. Everybody loves dogs. I'd have one myself except I can't in the apartment I'm in. I'd have ten. But a city's no place for a dog, anyway. It's not natural." Candace walked next to the man and his wagging dog, away down the sidewalk. She told him about dogs needing room to run and bark and do their business without being stared at, and the man was entirely agreeable. He didn't say a word.

After that, except for her nap and a sandwich, Candace worked all day at the warehouse. She sorted eggs by size and pointed-ness of end and glued them to cardboard, cleaned and polished car parts, painted other car parts. She ran the industrial ware-house fan at different speeds to determine the best undulations of pantyhose, and she rearranged some of those legs and their anchors for improved wave effects. She cut polka-dot cloth and stapled it to walls, and she pinned sheaves of it around her bodice and her head to make a sort of multilayered, multicol-ored, multidotted gown. Outside, she posted painted cardboard signs announcing her work-in-progress and inviting participa-tion, and when people did wander in, she offered them round bologna sandwiches and Cheerios and put them to work paint-ing or reclining behind the undulating waves of pantyhose while holding different combinations of polka-dot fabrics. She laid out an array of Salvation Army polka-dot dresses and had people choose and model them and tell her, into her tape recorder, what they thought about Chaos.

It was after dark when Candace cleaned her last brush and collected her signs and leftover bologna. On her way home, *shh-shh-shhing* along the street with her bag of foods in need of refrigeration, she was accosted by an agitated young man who demanded her money, watch, and jewelry.

"Are you crazy?" Candace said. "Jewelry?" In the poor light she thought that perhaps he'd mistaken the paint splatters around her neck and on her tunic as necklaces and brooches. She was definitely not parting with her nose ring. "Scat on out of here before I make you sorry. *And,* by the way, don't you know it's rude to pick on impoverished ladies with veins in their legs? Why don't you go rob a Brink's truck or something *manly?*"

The man backed up a couple of steps and moved his finger inside his shirt, trying to make her think he had a gun. "You do what I say or you'll be sorry," he said. "Put down that bag and cane and give me that money belt."

It wasn't a cane, exactly, that Candace was carrying. It was a buffalo penis bone made to be a cane, but she carried it more for these kinds of occasions. People with good sense didn't tend to bother her, but now and then she'd run into a hoodlum like tonight's, or she'd be called upon to help someone else in a situation, though certainly, despite what you might think, she didn't go around looking for situations. They just sometimes happened around her. She had taken to carrying her buffalo penis bone like someone else might carry a folded umbrella, just in case.

"Take that!" Candace yelled, banshee-like, as she swung the bone into the man's midsection. He fell back and she stepped forward, and she pounded him again, on one shoulder, then in the legs.

He dropped a gun, then cried out like he was choking and ran.

Candace picked up the gun. *Gosh-darn,* she thought. It was

the real thing. She thought about keeping it, but then decided guns were more trouble than they were worth. One less in the world would have to be an improvement. She dropped it through a sewer grate.

She knew she had not really hurt the young man, though she thought maybe she should have. The head of her buffalo penis bone, the part she had hit him with, was well padded with mink fur. She had only, mostly, scared him.

At home, when Candace only wanted to have some chamomile tea, toast, frozen lasagna, and Cheese Doodles with a movie channel, she found she had company. Her husband was in her bed.

He was her husband, technically. They were married, and they'd been married for four years. Bob was Algerian and had needed her help to stay in this country. She'd obliged.

"Wake up," she said. "What are you doing here?" She had changed the lock the last time she'd thrown him out, but now she was regretting leaving the key to the new lock on the little nail next to the molding. It did not take a genius, which Bob was not, to let himself in. She was also, at this moment, regretting dropping that gun into the sewer.

"Darling Candy," Bob said, sitting up. His dreadlocks, the front ones, fell over his face. "I was wondering where you were. I was worrying about you out there in the jungle, in this terrible dangerous neighborhood. Why don't you let me take you away from here?"

"Take me where?"

Bob shrugged. Of course he had nowhere to take her, and

no money. If he had a place to stay or food to eat, he wouldn't have come to Candace's. He didn't like her that much to put himself in her presence outside of a more-or-less emergency. "It's the thought that counts. Is it not?"

Candace went to the stove and made tea and toast, which she brought to Bob in bed. "One night," she said. "Then you go."

He fell back asleep almost immediately. He did not look good, Candace, sitting there on the edge of the bed, thought. The man was exhausted from whatever. She didn't know what he did. As brave as she was, she didn't want to know. She looked at the mahogany mask of his face and thought how beautiful he was, even in the folds of skin around his closed eyes, especially in the little laugh wrinkles beside his mouth. If she could make a face like that . . . She turned down the covers and looked at his hairless sculpted chest, the hollow at the breastbone, the nipples like perfect dark, pimpled circles. His chest moved with his breathing, with the pulse of his heart. She had two, not quite revelations, but serious, clear thoughts: A human, even an ugly one, is a work of art. And life, even a vague, underaccomplished one, is art, and the highest form of art/life is just getting through without causing harm.

Candace put her hand on her husband's chest, the pads of her four fingers over his heart. She felt his heart beat, regular, regular, skip-murmur, regular again, thump, thump. A chaotic behavior. She would have an audio portion to her installation. People talking about chaos, and then chaos, the arrhythmic beating of her husband's heart, while the pantyhose waves flowed, while the dots dotted, while the flower smells smelled. The whole work was coming together now in her mind. She would need heart monitoring equipment, Bob hooked up in a chair, other people too, listening to their own and each other's hearts and learning something about order and disorder, persistence, goodwill. There was still something misty in the conceptualization, but Candace was getting there, to what, when it was done, we might all see had to do not only with beauty and strength but with grace.

The Girl Who Dreamed Only Geese

S HE WOKE AT THE INSTANT the flock began to meet the water, amid the roar of wings sieving the air, the touch of stretched feet, the flop of white bellies. They rained down, as thick as pollen lighting on a lake—not specks but huge, fat-bodied birds, one after another, *splash, splash, splash, splash, splash*. She was within the tumult—not among the geese exactly, but somehow caught within the motion and the noise, as though her bodiless self was only a breath in the air being thrust down by powerful wings, being echoed across by the noises of feathers scraping air and water. More air spilled from long necks, out of parted bills with flickering tongues. The cackling, that hollow exuberance, fell all around her like chips.

Samantha lay in her narrow bed and wondered why she kept dreaming geese. Geese, in real life, were only those large birds that once, at a petting zoo ten or so years earlier, had run at her and, she thinks, would have nipped her had her mother not scooped her to safety. More recently, at Tule Lake with her scout troop, she'd seen the wild ones that wintered there, thousands of snow geese bathing and feeding. As a rule, she wasn't overly fond of birds, didn't pay any of them that much attention. She knew only the usual and obvious things about geese. She knew they flew in v-shaped formations, north in spring, south in fall. They were predictable like that.

The geese dreams, which had been coming unbidden for several nights, were disturbing to her. Always the geese were very near and very large, crashing down around her in a way that was not actually threatening but still uncomfortably close. They were always in motion, noisy, their feathers and thick bodies suggesting suffocation. The birds themselves seemed agitated, crowding one another, making all that clatter. She had no idea where they were coming from, what they wanted. She had, truly, no idea what they were doing in her dreams. They were completely unconnected to her life.

Samantha's life revolved largely around school, from which, now that she was in ninth grade, she carried home piles of books. Every evening she applied herself to these without being asked, and received, in return, consistent high grades and accolades. She wasn't all brains, though; she also played sports, volleyball all winter and now softball. She had plenty of friends, if not one she counted "best." She had a boyfriend, Chris, also her age, to whom she devoted considerable thought if not actual attention.

Birds were simply not part of her experience, not part of what she knew. What she knew included her home, with the dark old furniture that had belonged to great-grandparents, and her town, a long road away from the jostling of San Francisco. She could name every shop in the local mall and what each of her friends would order at McDonald's, Arby's, and Taco Bell. She knew, as well, that she had conflicting feelings about her father, who was living all the time now in Alaska, where he kept waiting for a good fishing season and meanwhile didn't seem to do much of anything. She knew, most worrisome of all, that her mother was dying of cancer, runaway cells that had started in a breast and were now growing a big, inoperable lump behind her liver.

NANCY LORD

When Samantha had gotten out of bed and washed her face, but before she dressed, and while the sounds and crowding of geese still lingered with her, she made cinnamon toast and carried a tray to her mother's room.

Her mother was awake, lying on her back and listening to very faint news on public radio. She pushed herself up with her elbows and gave Samantha her usual half-shy, half-beaming smile, the one that always made Samantha feel both loved and embarrassed, even burdened. Her mother, she knew, had felt from the very beginning that Samantha had been a great blessing and accomplishment; Samantha was, in her mother's opinion and despite evidence to the contrary, just about perfect. Her mother, adoring her so, felt bad not that she was so sick but that she couldn't cheer Samantha at games, take her hiking in the mountains, or teach her how to drive. Samantha was quite sure that her mother was less afraid of death than she was terrified about abandoning her daughter.

Samantha set the toast and juice on a hospital table that swung over the bed. She sat in the straight-backed chair beside the bed and ate her own toast.

"You need to eat more than that," her mother said. "Kathy brought some nice grapefruit. Please eat one. Or a banana."

"I will," Samantha said, knowing she wouldn't, knowing that her mother—the way she was chewing and chewing, working the toast around her mouth—was having trouble swallowing or even thinking of food. Her mother only ate because food was part of what was keeping her alive, and if she didn't maintain a reasonable weight, she would have to go back into the hospital to have nutrition dripped into her.

Her mother slid open the bedside drawer and took out

what she called her "paraphernalia." Samantha, looking away, only heard the cellophane wrappers tearing, the plastic parts being fitted. She looked at the poster on the wall—the tusked mammoth that advertised an anthropology conference her mother had attended years before—and only saw from the corner of her eye her mother reach inside her T-shirt to fish out her tube and plunge more painkiller into it. Her mother was good at this—as good as she'd been at troweling through archeological pits, or sewing Barbie clothes, or extracting splinters from Samantha's fingers. When she was still driving, she had given herself shots while she waited at stoplights, like it was nothing, like some other mother might run an emery board across her fingernails or change the radio station.

Samantha couldn't imagine the pain that made her mother shoot herself with drugs, more and more often now, as though she was on a clock that was speeding up. Her mother—who had never even liked to take aspirin—had always said, "If something hurts, your body's telling you to give it a rest. If you mask the pain, you're only going to hurt yourself more."

When Samantha looked back, her mother was already relaxing into her pillows. Her wasted arms were clasped now around her swollen belly. It hurt Samantha to see them—elbows and wrists like wooden knobs, the limbs between only bones with sagging, wrinkled, diseased-looking skin. And that belly—stretched like a drum, as though her mother were pregnant, but all of it just swelling, retained fluids, the tumor—mysteries even the doctors couldn't explain. Fat and thin in all the wrong places—her mother, who had been so beautiful. Samantha tried to smile at her mother, who was smiling back, her eyes shiny. Her face was so angular now, and her hair, mussed from sleeping, was thin and dull. But at least she had hair! Most of the women in her mother's cancer group wore wigs or turbans or went around bald; they envied any hair at all.

Samantha asked, "Can I get you something else?"

Her mother shook her head. "Sonya's going to be here in an hour."

Sonya was one of the women in her mother's support group—friends who made it possible for her mother to still be at home, and for Samantha to continue her more or less regular life. Sonya would help her mother do whatever she needed to do, and she'd drive her to a doctor's appointment. Later, someone else would bring a nice dinner for both of them and would set the table with candles and cloth napkins. Women came in to do laundry and other chores that Samantha herself could do perfectly well except that they never gave her a chance. They would drive her to a friend's or take her shopping or anything at all; she only had to call Jean, the woman in charge, who hadn't even been one of her mother's friends but had come out of nowhere to help. Samantha was grateful for everything Jean, Sonya, Marla, Elizabeth, Tory, and Kathy did, but on the other hand, there was something about being an object of all their goodwill that depressed her, or made her feel less capable than she thought she should be. She didn't want to be a charity case.

Her mother wanted to know if she had clean clothes and what was happening after school and did she have a ride home, and then it was time for Samantha to dress and gather her books. She stopped in her mother's room once more before she left, to touch her lips to her mother's hot cheek. Her mother gave her another of those looks so full of drugged-up love.

Samantha could only think that once she got to school, her classmates would be talking about their parents yelling at them for the way they were dressed or wore their hair, and Samantha would have nothing to say. She would never tell anyone, "My mother thinks I'm perfect," just as she never said, "My mother's dying." Those were the two unspeakables.

That night she again dreamed geese. The geese were on water—a lakey, swampy green-water place full of grasses and cattails. They were eating, ducking their long necks under, tipping their squat tails into the air. They were all so white and plump and buoyant. Beneath the water, their pink feet pedaled effortlessly. Water poured off their backs and sides as though they were carved from wax. They turned their heads—dark eye, dark eye, dark eye. They weren't looking at her; they just *were*. Their eyes weren't mean or kind or anything other than alert. Samantha could smell the water, that fresh smell that was like wind, that was meant to be inhaled deeply; to breathe it was like drinking it. The geese were so purely white, swimming in circles, high on the water, dripping from black-lined bills the same pink as their legs.

Samantha felt something expand in her own chest. She couldn't say what. It was the smell of water, the plumpness of goose, a featherweightness of some kind of yearning or want or need—something that left her, when she woke, both calm and, not knowing for what, wishful.

On Sunday evening, her father called, as he generally did once a month if he remembered, interrupting the video watching she

NANCY LORD

and her mother shared on Sundays, when the video store rented two new films for the price of one. Two-for-one video watching was one of their small economies, and something they did together, though her mother often fell asleep in the middle, or, when the pain came, sucked her teeth in a way that was distracting. This time when her father called, Samantha motioned to her mother to keep on watching, but her mother stopped the video and watched TV instead—something stupid on *60 Minutes*. Samantha knew she was actually eavesdropping. Her mother pretended that she didn't much care about Samantha's father anymore, or that she cared only that he would catch some fish and make his settlement and support payments, but Samantha knew there was more to it than that.

Her father had his fake-cheerful voice. "Hey, kiddo, how're things with you?"

"Fine."

"School going OK?"

"Yeah."

Samantha knew she should offer more than one-word answers, but she honestly didn't have a lot to say to her father. "What're *you* up to?" she asked. "Still got snow?"

"Yeah, but it's going fast. Saw my first mosquito today."

Samantha tried to picture Seward, Alaska. It had been several years since she'd been there. Mostly she remembered the boat harbor and the big mountain behind town that people raced up and down every July 4th. She didn't know what to say about mosquitoes. She didn't remember them from Seward, which was not to say they hadn't been there. She said something about softball and asked if he'd gotten the picture she sent—the one that had been in the paper, of her with the school chorus.

He remembered it then and thanked her. She could think of nothing else to tell him and felt bad that she couldn't, but then she wondered why she was the one who was supposed to be bubbling over with information. For an instant she felt sorry for her father—sorry that he felt such obligation for her, that he had to call her, that he had to send money he didn't have.

"So how's your mother doing?" he asked.

"OK," she lied. "We're watching a movie."

"What one?"

"*Bullets Over Broadway*. Woody Allen. It's funny."

"Don't think I've seen it. Well, you take care. Remember, you're always welcome to come up here for the summer or whatever. I could really use you on the boat."

"I'm pretty busy here," Samantha said.

"Well, let me know if you need anything."

She went back to the couch. Her mother restarted the movie. "How's your father?" she asked, but she was already watching the screen.

"Same," Samantha said. "He asked for you." She was thinking, *if you need anything.* She did need something, very badly. She needed a healthy mom. A mom who wouldn't die. As if her father could do anything about that.

~

For several nights she didn't dream at all, or if she did dream, she didn't remember, when she woke, what she'd dreamt. Geese, though, followed her through her days, evenings, the times when she lay awake at night. At school, when she thought she was listening to her biology teacher go on about mitosis and meiosis, she realized she was really feeling cushioned by large, feathery, fatty goose bodies. When she opened her locker, she heard a distant and high-pitched yelping she knew was a gaggle of geese somewhere in the middle of her head. After dinner, when she washed dishes, the water from the faucet brought that lake smell back to her, and she had a vision of pink feet paddling. She watched her mother fall asleep on the couch, her head buried in a pillow and her fists clamped between her knees, and she thought of geese sleeping with their heads tucked under wings, their full and buoyant bodies floating on calm and gently lapping water. In bed, she imagined wings unfolded like fans over her and felt, again, the embrace of thick, silencing down.

Her mother got sicker. She went into the hospital, where she was laid out under a white sheet and hooked to an IV bag. She was thinner than ever, nearly disappearing under the flat sheet except for the bulge of her belly. Every evening one or another member of the support group brought Samantha to visit and then spent the night at the house with her.

Samantha could see that her mother tried very hard in her presence to look animated and cheerful but that she was exhausted and sometimes confused. When Samantha held her hand, she felt the pulse throbbing through it like something desperate to keep up. People brought flowers and dolls and cards with photographs of beautiful gardens and wild places, and her mother's hospital room began to look like its own gift shop. Samantha was glad that her mother had so many people who cared about her. What she didn't like was having them look at her, Samantha, with furrowed brows and pursed lips. She didn't like overhearing by accident, which she did more than once, people feeling sorry for her and wondering what was to become of her. What was to become of her was that, when her mother died, she would go live with her legal guardian, Kathy, who lived nearby. She would continue at the same school and not be disrupted. This had all been planned a long time ago. The other option was for her to live with her father, although she had not been enthusiastic about this and neither, she thought, had he.

At school or with her friends, she didn't talk about her mother. If someone asked, she just said, "She's in the hospital." Mostly people didn't ask. Instead, she would see them looking at her. They already knew. Sometimes someone said, "I'm sorry your mother's in the hospital." Then she said, "Thank you."

Her boyfriend, Chris, talked mostly about cars and music. They walked places together or he got his older brother to drive them to concerts and music stores. A few times he met her outside the hospital, but he never offered to go in. He said he didn't like hospitals. He told jokes. Samantha liked him for telling stupid jokes and for not asking her how she felt about anything.

Samantha didn't tell Chris, or anyone, about the geese. She might have, if she'd known what to think about them, but all she really had were impressions. She couldn't have described what the geese looked like, exactly, and she didn't even know if they were a real kind of geese or only a concept that existed in her head. Or not even in her head. They were just sort of *there*—on the edge of everything.

If she could have said something about them, it would only have been that she was sure that they were geese, white geese with pink bills and legs, faint and pastel at the same time that they were large and close, almost bulky. It wasn't that they *did*

NANCY LORD

anything or that in her dreams she did anything with them, either. She wasn't sure if she was even *with* them in her dreams, or if she was just seeing them, like through glass. It was all very vague to her, vague and somehow agreeable. Solid and soft and dreamy all at the same time, not there and there, a vision completely without explanation. The one consistent thing was that the geese were never in flight; always they were near water, either landing on it or swimming and feeding or fluttering around.

Neighbors brought food. A teacher gave her a book about bad things happening to good people. People were nice to her. They lowered their voices around her. Her grandparents and her mother's sister called from the East Coast. She talked to them about her mother and school and the weather. She would say, "It's been rainy," while she was thinking not about rain or her mother or whoever she was talking to, but about geese. And not *about* geese, either. It was not conscious like that. There would just be geese in her head, big and soft and white, with their dark eyes, taking up space.

Her father sent her mother a card with a picture of wildflowers. On the inside was printed *get well soon*. Her mother was not going to get well. Maybe, Samantha hoped, she could get *better* enough to come home again, but she was not going to get *well*. She was pretty sure her father knew that and had made an unfortunate Hallmark choice. Or, probably, where he shopped there wasn't much to choose from.

At night, when she undressed in her room, she looked at herself in the mirror. Her breasts were round and, she thought, nice-looking. She liked them. She liked to touch them sometimes, to hold them in her hands. She liked the way they felt to her hands and she liked the way they felt when she squeezed them just a little; they felt full and a little achy, sexy.

She looked at her body and touched herself, then put her hands over both breasts and pushed them flat.

She found, in her dresser, her thickest flannel nightgown.

That night and for the next two, Samantha dreamed only geese. Even before she fell asleep, she expected them, their featherweightedness and all the swirling water that surrounded them. She had come to count on their unruffled plainness and white-noise cackling.

The geese carried into her waking life, softening her steps through the house, easing her through her studies, edging into her voice when she spoke in class. She batted better than ever at softball and surprised herself by picking up grounders that had previously bounced past her; somehow, she had gotten both stronger and more agile.

Near the end, her grandparents, her aunt, and her mother's oldest friend flew in. Samantha went to the airport with Kathy to meet them. The plane was late, and she and Kathy waited by a window where they could see planes taking off and landing. Some of them were small, single-engine planes, and they made Samantha think of birds, especially when they got small in the sky. She thought of geese and of their heavy bodies, which didn't seem like they ought to be able to hang in the air, any more than airplanes should. She heard in her head the papery sound of geese wings folding and unfolding, the scratch of feathers being preened.

Kathy gave her a look. "You doing OK?"

"Yes," Samantha said. She knew she was supposed to be thinking about her mother, and what it meant that the whole family was gathering. "I was . . . remembering some geese."

"Did you see some here?"

"No."

"There used to be a lot around the airport, but they were considered a hazard, so they were all killed or something. Chased away, maybe. They could get sucked into a plane's engine."

Samantha thought about that. The absence of geese. It was like a big hole, a blank, an empty space. She didn't understand how there could be geese and then not geese. And how most people wouldn't even know the difference. She didn't know there'd been airport geese, and she hadn't missed them. Now she wanted them back. If they were a hazard, let the airplanes go somewhere else.

"It was wetlands here," Kathy was saying. "That's why they built the airport here. All that room, and all they had to do was dump some gravel."

Samantha knew she was being irrational. She thought she might be allowed to be irrational, but not about geese.

Kathy pointed out sacks of mail being loaded onto a plane, and then a jet landed and headed for their gate.

Her grandparents, her aunt, and her mother's best friend all cried when they saw Samantha. Samantha let herself be hugged and kissed, but she felt like her head was stuffed with feathers.

They were all there, with Samantha's mother, when she died. Her mother was with them, talking weakly and squeezing hands, and then she was unconscious and still with them, and then she was gone and only her ironed-flat body with its one stubborn swelling was left beneath the sheet.

That night, in the houseful of sleeping relatives, Samantha again dreamed geese. Only this time, the geese were flying. Their wings swept up and down with heavy, powerful strokes that pressed and pushed against the air as though it were a solid, soupy thing. The geese themselves were stretched out, necks extended, legs tucked, beating and beating the air and barking their calls. Wing feathers extended like the fingers of open hands, every hollow stem, every fiber and barb catching light. Heads rocked forward rhythmically, like those of galloping horses. They were a great flock, lined out across pale blue sky in one of those long, whispery, scraggling v's, and the earth was very far below, a floating blue billiard ball.

When Samantha woke in the dark, with the little bit of street light coming through the opening in her curtain, she was breathing to the beat of wings. Sitting partway up, she looked around at the familiar gray shapes of her dresser, the worn armchair with clothes thrown over it, her desk with its curved-neck lamp and stack of books. She listened to a throaty snore from the living room, the rattle of the refrigerator, her clock's ticking, and—from somewhere far away—a sound like geese honking, getting fainter, fainter. And then there was nothing, just a place in her mind that was like the far side of the moon.

She lay back down. Her clock kept ticking; something in

NANCY LORD

the house creaked. Already, she missed the geese. She missed them because she'd grown accustomed to them, as she'd grown accustomed to so much else.

She lay awake a long time, but when at last she slept, it was with the sure knowledge that there were, sometime to come, other dreams.

The Census Taker

Anton Chekhov to would-be biographers:
"If there are no facts, substitute something lyrical."

I T WAS THE SUMMER of 1890, though Darya had already stopped keeping track of the years, when the visitor came to Sakhalin Island. They called him Doctor Chekhov, and they said he was a writer.

He went out in the evening, and Darya cleared away his supper dishes. Everywhere around his chair he'd set down stacks of white cards. She looked at them and saw that they were all the same, blocks of Russian letters and blank spaces. One small pile had been filled in with black, cursive writing, as snarled and twiny as grapevines, and as mysterious.

She stood, a thin aging woman with faded, green-tinged hair and rounded shoulders, in the doorway to the adjoining room. How neatly he'd unpacked and arranged his belongings in the small space! His blankets were wrapped tightly around the husk mattress, the top of the crisp sheet folded back. A few articles of dark clothing hung from a pole at the end of the room over a well-traveled trunk. On the bedside table, atop a bit of lace runner, lay a small photo of a woman in an oval frame, a thimble-sized glass for taking doses of medicine, a pince-nez case, and two sturdy leather books, one of which lay open across the other. The books smelled of pipe smoke, and the lace runner, creased into valleys and low ridges from its folding, was as white as a swan's feathers. Darya stroked the back of her hand over the writer's own blankets, not mean little prison blankets stinking of camphor and old sweat but luxurious spreads that still felt of natural sheep oil and smelled faintly of sun and warm, dry places.

Her heart swelled as though it would burst, and Darya flung herself onto the narrow bed. She clutched the thick wool in her hands and buried her nose against it. She cried and sobbed and would have rubbed the skin right off her hardened face, would have wound herself in those sweet blankets for life. She reached for the photograph of the woman and held it against her pounding chest, and she took in her other hand the leather pince-nez case that was so finely made, so elegant, and she pulled the two books onto the bed and caressed their covers and turned their pages, and breathed their drawing-room scent.

An observer might have thought Darya had lost her mind, or that she was in desperate love with the man, the writer who had come to Sakhalin. Alone in the small log house, she howled like a woman in mad, desperate love, a woman who would suffocate herself in her lover's clothing, or cut out her heart with the jagged edge of his medicine cup.

But in fact Darya had met Chekhov only an hour or two before, when she'd been assigned as his servant. She was as indifferent to him as she was to any man.

She clutched the blankets and the frame and case and books, and then the lace runner that some kind woman's fingers had embroidered, and what she cried for was only the fact that these things existed, and that they had come so recently from Russia. They still carried the air of Russia with them, and the dust, and the fingerprints of honest people. She, on the other hand, who loved Russia so well, with all her wronged heart and her soul, was banished from it forever.

She had, she'd always thought, a gift for the dramatic.

He didn't notice, when he returned, that she'd been crying, and she hoped that everything in his room was as it had been, the blankets taut across the mattress, the books arranged as before. He took off his overcoat and hung it on a hook behind the door, and then he sat in his chair and picked up a blank card. "Shall we do a card on you?"

"It's for you to say."

Chekhov fixed her with a slightly quizzical look, not unkind, through the circles of his pince-nez. His hair had been ruffled by the wind so that instead of lying flat, a part of it stuck up on top like a tipsy stack of hay, and another lock curled just to the side of one eye. He was, she thought, quite a handsome man, tall and springy, but he looked at this moment a little pinched in the spaces around his trimmed beard. "It's my intention," he said, "to complete a card on every person on the island—that is, every convict, every settler, every free person and child. Aside from cooking for me, I'd like it if you'd accompany me sometimes to the prisons and the homes, particularly when I'm to speak with women and children."

"Yes sir." She thought she ought to curtsy or somehow show respect, but it had been so long since she'd known anything but being ordered about, or shouted at, or worse, and her gray convict's smock and leggings were not the kind of clothing to be plucked at. She lowered her head and looked at the floor in front of her ugly men's shoes.

"Please sit."

She sat on the edge of a low stool.

He dipped his pen into ink, and the sound, as the nib hit the side of the bottle, was like a small bell. From the street she could hear the weary feet of men dragging home from the mines, the rattle of fetters.

"Name?"

Darya gave her name, her current address, her birthdate, her birthplace not far from the Volga, the date of her conviction, and her sentence.

"Your crime?"

"I'm here because of my husband."

"And is your husband here, too?"

"He is dead."

The pen scratched on the card.

"Why are you here because of your husband?"

"Because I killed him."

"I see." He did not look up until he had finished writing, but when he did, his face looked merely thoughtful. "I understand that half of the prisoners on the island are murderers."

"I put a kitchen knife in his chest," she said.

"Twenty years ago."

"Yes." She began again to cry. "For all the rest of my living life, I have to stay on this wretched, wretched island." She snuffled into a rag and noticed that he had put down his pen and was not going to tell her any different. "They say you're a writer," she said.

He hesitated and then said, "I am, but I'm not. I'm here merely to take a census, a count of all the people on the island."

"Will you write about me? Put me in a book?"

He tapped the card he'd just written. "I've got your information."

"It was a very large kitchen knife. I took it in both my hands like this." She demonstrated—how she'd held the wooden handle in front of her, how her fisted-together hands had shaken, how she'd plunged the blade again and again. "There was a sucking and squishing noise," she said. She tried to imitate it with her lips, that sound of air sucking in and out of her man's opened lungs, the gurgling of hot blood that had been so much, and so red. "I would do it again," she said. She crossed herself.

Chekhov got up from his chair, a little stiff, she thought, for someone so young. "You'll have breakfast for me in the morning?"

"A famous writer like you, sir, it's an honor." She wrapped herself in her shawl, tossing the tattered ends back around her with a flourish.

Soon after, when she climbed under her own foul blankets on the cold stove of the hut she shared with her cohabitant and another family, she lay awake for a long time with a hand over her face. When she pinched her nostrils just right, she could still smell the sun-drenched fields of Mother Russia, with a very faint honeyed whiff of far-off linden trees. She could see herself there, like seeing herself in a play. She could see herself in a costume gown, with a shiny sequined purse. As she faded off into sleep, the two strands—of life in Russia and life in a play, one that might be written by her new, serious employer—wound themselves together until they were the same barely imaginable thing.

The next day, Darya accompanied Chekhov to the prison barracks.

"Anton Pavlovich," she said, slogging along the muddy road beside him. Overhead the sky was nearly as black as beach coal and spit needles of hard rain. Smoke permeated the settlement with a gritty closeness, as though the oppressive sky was keeping it from rising, holding it thick and choking against the ground. "Anton Pavlovich," she said again, taking him by the elbow. "They're not so interesting in the prison. It's only the free women there, the ones that came with their husbands."

"Yes, yes," he said. "We'll talk to everyone." His bag, heavy with cards, swung from his shoulder.

Inside the prison, the air was still smoky and smelled as well of sour sleep and dirty, wet clothing. The men were all out at labor, and only women and children were inside, lying idly on the communal plank bed that ran down the center of the ward or attending to their clothes or themselves in the poor light. A pig wandered across the crusty, spit-stained floor, and several babies whimpered as though they didn't have the strength to cry out.

Chekhov started at one end. He stood while he asked his questions, and the women answered, this one married to a counterfeiter, that one to a man, she said, wrongly convicted of murder. The children scratched at themselves and looked blank when Chekhov asked them direct questions about their ages and birthplaces.

Darya stood to one side, holding his bag, handing him new cards and taking the filled ones. She waved the cards, as she'd seen him do, to dry the ink, and then she traced over the mysterious black writing with the point of her finger, recreating the

NANCY LORD

loops and swirls and the tight hard circles with her own smooth, rhythmic motions. She only half-listened to the dreary droning of the next watery-eyed woman, whose husband had beaten another man to death and given her eleven children, of whom four lived with them in the prison. She thought instead of her own lost life, which might be transformed by the hands of an artist. Cultivated people would read her story; they would say, "that Darya . . ." But what would they say? She was not clear about the details. That was the work of an artist.

Chekhov passed her a completed card. Waving it, she observed how much more ink it had than the others, than her own from the night before. Chekhov had even turned it sideways, written up the long side of it in a smaller, thickened script. Darya eyed the woman to whom it belonged; she was undistinguished, a potato-eating peasant with dull hair. What made her so interesting? In a fit of jealousy, she jammed the card into Chekhov's bag, felt the edge of it crunch up against hard leather. She listened to him question a young girl she knew for a fact had worked as a prostitute for a half-dozen years already, and her mother and sisters did the same, and when she took that completed card from him, she was glad to see how much white space remained, how little there was to tell about that simple, boring one. In another part of the room Chekhov asked kindly questions of a small girl with tangled hair. She told him she was six years old and had come to Sakhalin with her father. She said something else in a soft, meek voice.

"Speak up there," Darya instructed her. "The gentleman can't hear you."

The small girl looked at her and repeated, "I hold my

papa's chains when he walks."

When they left the barracks and were making their way back along the rutted road, Chekhov wore a pained expression.

Darya told him again, "Those aren't very interesting women. After all, they didn't commit crimes of their own. They only came here to be with their men." She stepped around a large puddle. "They didn't have to come. Now me, there was no other place safe enough for me. Too dangerous, a woman that would sink a knife thirty-two times into a man, 'til he was chopped meat. Did I tell you I broke the tip off that knife, hitting bone? The guards were all frightened of me." She went on, telling about the first prison she was in, the guards she had threatened, the judge she had threatened, the shackles she'd been placed in.

After a time he interrupted her. "Can you imagine?" he said. "That tiny little girl, first her father kills her mother, then he brings her all the way out here, keeps her with him in that miserable tubercular room where everyone sleeps together on a pile of lice-infested rags. She holds his chains."

"I didn't have anyone to hold my chains," Darya said. "Had to hold 'em myself. And I'm not a strong woman, as you can see."

The next day, as they began rounds of the settlers' huts, she asked, "What did you write, sir?"

Chekhov seemed to come back from somewhere deep in his thoughts. "About?"

"To make you a famous writer."

He smiled. "I don't know how famous. Mostly I write little sketches, stories, mostly comic things."

"Funny?" She didn't think he seemed very funny.

"Sometimes not very funny. Or funny and not-funny." After a minute he added, "Someone once said my writing is about the inability of human beings to communicate with one another."

"I know all about that," she said.

But he was on to something else, saying something about the settlers, those men who'd completed their prison sentences and were free to live in a place of their own, so long as they didn't leave the island. He had noticed already that, since settlers no longer received prison rations, they were often worse off than the prisoners, unless they were good at something, like gambling. "Now these women," Chekhov said. "Some are settlers themselves, some are free women who accompanied their husbands, and some are convicts who are simply allowed to live with settlers instead of being imprisoned. Am I right?"

"Like me," Darya said.

"Cohabitants," Chekhov said.

She could tell he was trying to ask politely how this worked. Since there weren't very many women on the island, they had a certain value. They could be used to keep house and work in the fields, as well as in the obvious way. "Like fishes swimming upstream," she said, trying to also be polite.

"Excuse me?"

"When the steamers arrive, the women are like fishes. They go off the ship, and first the officials get their pick, and then the clerks and guards, and then the settlers get what's left. Picked off, like fishes in a creek."

"I see," he said, and they were at the door of their first hut.

The woman, nursing a bluish baby, barely stirred when they entered, and the room had a foul vomity smell. She gave her information timidly, each response ending like a question, as though she wasn't sure if her answers were the ones wanted or if they might earn her a beating. She wasn't sure how many children she had—three living, she said once, and then named four, and then she said she'd left twin daughters behind in Sverdlovsk and only God knew what had become of them. Darya watched a brown-shelled beetle crawl along a crack in the floor; when it reached her, she crushed it with her heel and ground it into dust. "Just killing one of your bugs, dear," she said to the woman, who hadn't seemed to notice.

Darya knew the toothless woman in the next house. She had come to Sakhalin on a transport not long after Darya, and they had once fought over part of a pickled fish. Darya fumed while Chekhov, one leg across the other, his foot jiggling, asked his questions and filled out his card. The woman said she had come from Perm, which Darya knew was a lie. She was really from Okhansk, an insignificant settlement where nothing had ever happened except that the woman's husband got drunk and knocked another man to the ground. "My husband and I killed a gentleman," the woman said.

"He was no gentleman," Darya corrected. "The way I heard it, he was a drunk, just like your husband, and you didn't have nothing to do with it."

The woman's face reddened. "It was an accident," she said, "but we was afraid. We left him in a ditch, and then he drowned. They said it was murder. I pushed his face in the water."

"You just say that to try to make yourself important." Darya glared. "It was your man did all that."

The woman looked at Darya and then back at Chekhov, who sat with poised pen. "The court found I pushed his face in the water."

"Did not!" shouted Darya.

"Did too! What do you know?" The woman, sputtering, sprayed a mist of saliva into the space between them.

"I know I didn't do nothing like watch some poor drunk man drown. I did mine with a knife." Darya mimed holding a knife like a sickle and slashing it back and forth. "I killed a man in cold blood. He deserved it, too."

Chekhov cleared his throat. "Ladies," he said. "I'd like to finish the interview."

"I tell you, she's just trying to make herself interesting, and she's not, not at all. She's common." Darya turned to face the log wall, where labels from bottles were pasted up for something to look at. When Chekhov handed her the completed card, she was pleased to see how little writing it actually held.

⁓

Another morning, when Darya arrived at Chekhov's hut in the rain, he was still in his dressing gown and holding his head.

"I had a terrible night," he said. "All night I kept hearing these moaning noises, like people in pain. Someone kept saying, "My God, my God, my God.""

Darya readied the samovar, clonking and clunking utensils together, banging down a pitcher so that the noise of it caused Chekhov to wince. "It's the wind," she said.

When they finally left the hut, a group of prisoners was standing in the street outside a warehouse, ankle-deep in mud. Every scrap of their clothing was soaking wet, and rain ran down their faces like water over squashes. They were all shivering and hugging themselves, and a puffy-faced guard was rattling his keys and shouting, "Sure I'll give you a ticket. I'll give you a ticket you won't forget."

"I'm sick," one complained hoarsely. "My legs are all buckley." The front and sides of him were coated with mud. Another pressed swollen hands to his chest, while a third, his face grossly contorted, was doubled over with pain.

"My God, my God, my God," a man in the back groaned.

Darya turned to Chekhov, who had stopped in his tracks. "They want to go to the hospital," she said.

"Won't the guard let them?"

"Ha!" She kept going, picking her way through the mud as best she could. After a minute, Chekhov followed. Even to the corner, they could hear the guard ordering the men to move, and the one crying out, "My God, oh my God."

Darya took Chekhov's arm. "Now don't you be bothering yourself about that."

⌒

On another of their passes through the settlement, a group of waiflike children shot past them to scramble in a field, some running wildly, others slashing the air with the stiff hollow stalks of last year's pushki plants. Chekhov paused as though he was delighted to at last see children enjoying themselves.

"You know what they're playing, don't you?" Darya asked.

Chekhov glanced at her. "No. Is it a particular game?"

"The ones in the front's the escaped prisoners. The ones with the sticks, they's the guards."

They watched for a minute, and Darya said, "They say you write plays."

"I had a rather successful one produced a couple of years

ago." He was still looking at the children. "Maybe I'll write more."

"Maybe you will," Darya said. She was thinking very hard, *and put me in it*. She was seeing herself, again, in a gown, on a stage, with her hand flying to her brow the way once, so long ago, she'd seen an actress in a street fair make her grand gestures.

Just at that moment, one of the boys yelled out, "You'll hang for that," and whipped his stalk into a fence post so hard that the parasol head of it flew off into a ditch.

They returned to the main prison building, this time to the convict women incarcerated there, the few who were too dangerous to live outside the walls as servants or cohabitants. "A bunch of poisoners," Darya hissed. "I wouldn't give a kopeck for the lot of 'em."

Chekhov, as methodically as always, filled a card on each woman, even the ones who wouldn't give their true names or whose eyes wandered the walls as though they would never know where they were, or why. Darya just kept shaking her head.

Chekhov seemed most interested in the woman everyone called The Golden Hand. Darya had heard of her for years and was secretly pleased to be able to look her over. The woman's rough, renowned hands, on this occasion, sat in her lap, politely cupped together.

The Golden Hand offered her history to Chekhov, who wrote rather furiously to capture it. She told how she'd used her sexual charms to seduce lecherous guards, how she'd escaped prisons in Siberia three times and murdered innocent people four times. One of her victims had been a soldier, and she'd dressed in his clothes and passed that way for half a year.

It seemed to Darya that the woman went on and on with far too much pride for someone wedded to a cannonball she could barely drag across the cold floor. She began to fidget with the buttons on the side of her smock, and then to yawn and pat her mouth. Did anyone really care that this woman had smashed the skull of a peasant in order to steal his horse, or that she'd swum across a frigid Siberian river? Chekhov turned the card and began to write on its back side, the first time ever Darya had seen him do this. She crossed her arms on her chest and shuffled her feet with as much noise as she could make, and she stared hard at The Golden Hand. Even in the poor light she could make out her rather prominent mustache. It would have taken no special trick for such a woman to pass as a man.

They left the prison soon after. It was still raining, though not as hard, and Chekhov seemed distracted, squinting through the drips. "She don't even know where she comes from," Darya said, speaking of The Golden Hand. "Least I know I've got good Cossack blood. Us Cossacks are fighters. We don't sneak around. We don't pretend to be what we're not. When you put me in your book, Anton Pavlovich, say that. You might want to make some more writings about me. When I told you before, I didn't know you well and I didn't tell you about the other I did."

Chekhov kept walking. He didn't ask about the other, and so Darya continued. "I stabbed him all those times, same as I told you. But also I cut off his part. You know. That man's part." She made a slicing sound in the back of her throat. "Fell on the floor like that, like a piece of sausage."

"She was kind of a pathetic thing, wasn't she?" Chekhov

said. "Not what I expected. I thought she looked rather like a mouse."

Darya opened her mouth to protest, and then she didn't. She satisfied herself with this: the good writer had called that awful mustached woman only a mouse.

⁓

Darya sat on the riverbank and waited for Chekhov, who was completing yet another card in a hut just visible through the trees. The water, flowing past in slowly swirling patterns, was gray. The sky was gray. The eroded bank was gray, and so were the trees and their shagging bark. Even the riverside flowers— the stunted star-shaped blossoms clinging close to the sandy soil—were less purple than gray, as though a layer of dust lay over them. Darya tossed single pebbles into the water and listened to their *plok, plok, plok.* From across the river she heard the sounds of men cutting wood in the forest—axes thunking into wet wood, saws two-toning back and forth like someone with troubled breath, curses. The crash of a felled tree shook the earth beneath her. The smell of smoke was all around, but it wasn't enough to cover the stink of a skeletal fish that lay on the bank, half in and half out of the water, thirty feet away.

At last Chekhov came along the path and sat beside her.

She sighed and began to talk about herself, how many long years she'd been in exile, how wicked she was. She crossed herself and told him again how she had laughed when she maimed her old husband, and that it was her Cossack blood that made her so wild. "When I'm in your book," she said, "people will say, 'Darya Vladimirova, now that was a very interesting woman with a story to tell.' In Moscow, do you think, and in Saint

Petersburg, they'll read about me, they'll say 'that Darya Vladimirova, now, she was something?'"

"It's hard to say," Chekhov said.

She reached across the bag he'd set between them and clutched his arm. "But you'll write about me?"

"Inevitably," he said.

She sighed and balled her hands together in the lap of her smock. Some writer! He parceled out words like there were only so many and when he'd used them all, they'd be gone. *Yes* and *no* he'd already used, or he was saving.

"Look." Chekhov pointed at the sky.

At first there was only the same gray sky, but then she saw the bird glide from behind tall trees. It was only a seagull, gray and white with a pale yellow bill. An ordinary bird, it flapped its wings, looked their way, coasted by. She looked at Chekhov look at the bird, and what she saw was an ordinary man wearing a hat, and with a feathery little beard that left two bare places under his lower lip, to either side of the middle. He was not a well man, she thought; he was the consumptive type, and he was too easily distracted by a simple thing like a bird.

"If I had a gun I could shoot that," she said.

He looked at her, and she could read nothing at all in his expression.

"But of course I will never have a gun."

"That you won't."

"All right, then," she said, as she tugged her shift over her knees and flattened the cloth. She meant, what she did not say, that it wouldn't matter to her if the facts of her life were reduced to her name and dates on a white card, because, in fact, her life was her own and she *was* the star, and maybe

NANCY LORD

Doctor Chekhov, important as he was, was only a character in her own story, which might be funny, and might not, however she wanted it to be.

Why Owls Die with Wings Outspread

THE WAY JEREMY'S MOTHER PUT IT, he was living now with the only two people in the world who had ever tried to kill him. One was Claire, who, when they lived together before, had shot at him and only got a little flesh of his thigh. The other was, of course, himself.

He was not so sure that there weren't, in his twenty-eight years of dangerous living, other people who had tried to kill him. There was, for example, a fat kid in grammar school who had heaved a very large rock at him. A truck once had brushed his leg as he was bicycling along the side of a road, and he was pretty sure he saw evil intent in the driver's eyes. Most recently, a landlord did something to the furnace to give him headaches. He did not count threats from certain people to whom he owed money or the crossfire he had once innocently entered in a not-very-good neighborhood of Phoenix.

Regardless, he could understand his mother's concern. It was probably not good chemistry to put him and Claire together. They worked on one another like . . . well, he had never taken chemistry per se, but he *had* had a toy chemistry set, and he *had* tried his darndest to put things together that would explode, so he knew something about that. Nevertheless, he felt there was something inevitable in their relationship.

For one thing, they looked alike. Not that he looked like a girl, or Claire like a guy. But they were both long-boned and thin-waisted, with firmly jawed faces and similarly green eyes. Their hair was almost the same shade of brown, and straight, though Jeremy had recently, after getting his caught in a motor, chopped short the rest of what hadn't been yanked. Claire wore a ring through one unplucked eyebrow, and he had a hole in one ear. People sometimes took them for brother and sister. Whatever—Jeremy suspected he and Claire, on some level of twinnishness, deserved one another.

＜＝＝＝／

They were making a new start, and this meant moving to the mountains, where they would learn to be self-sufficient and not get mixed up in the bad business of the rest of the world.

On the first day they swept out the old cabin they'd found, carrying out whole nests of baby mice to relocate in a rotted woodpile. Both of them had a fondness for small animals, and even the spiders were given a solicitous evacuation. They cleaned leaves from the spring box, hung a cannabis-leaf flag from a pole they planted in the yard, and made a jug of sun tea. Jeremy climbed up on the roof and nailed a piece of tin over a hole, and Claire picked wildflowers for a table arrangement and measured windows for curtains.

On the second day they picked broken glass out of the yard and sorted through a stack of moldy magazines, mostly *Field & Stream,* from the cabin. They argued over who should wash their pot and plastic bowls and whether soap was necessary or environmentally unwarranted. They ate the last of their bread.

On the third day they drove the long dusty road down the mountain and bought fresh milk and flashlight batteries, then spent the rest of the afternoon and evening in the local bar. When they left that night they had no money, almost no gas in the truck, and half a quart of soured milk. They drove around through the town's dark streets looking for a cat that might appreciate even scuzzy milk, and they talked, with loud, excited, alcoholic enthusiasm, about an idea that had come to them, unbidden, in the bar.

Jeremy, had he been sober, might have recognized that he was falling again into a familiar pattern. His best ideas always came at alcoholic heights, and in the end they usually proved to have some small but fatal flaw. This had been the case when he'd decided he could make a living spearing fish in Hawaii, and he had spent borrowed money to get to Hawaii and buy a spear gun before he realized he got too claustrophobic under the water and didn't swim that well anyway, even with flippers. He'd also forgotten that, as a vegetarian, he really didn't want to kill fish. Unfortunately, no one was willing to pay him to just point out how pretty the fish were.

The whole problem with the American economic system, in the first place, was precisely that it was all about taking things, destroying them, ruining everything. Jeremy was committed to nonviolence, a concept he extended to trees, weeds, a shark that once tried to bite him, even things that other people might throw into a trash compacter but he could find another use for.

It was ironic, he knew, that he'd himself been the victim of violent attacks, by, as his mother was quite correct in putting it, the two people with whom he now lived. Both instances were explainable. In the case of Claire, they never should have had that .44 magnum sitting around the apartment. It just invited trouble. They never would have had it except it belonged to a friend who sometimes stayed with them and who tended to be a bit paranoid himself, given his line of work. It was just the wrong chemistry again: one pissed-off woman, one loaded gun, one guy (himself) too drunk to get out of the way.

The other occasion was nothing he was proud of, either, although anger had not been a part of it. He'd just been so incredibly *sad*. He was depressed, and his self-prescribed treatments had acted together in all the wrong ways to take him so far down he'd wanted only that it all end. Of course, as soon as he took the knife to his wrists, the sight of all that bubbling bright blood had sickened him, which is perhaps what saved him. What he threw up helped clear his system enough that he was able to stagger to the hallway. The last thing he remembered was trying to keep his cut wrists above the hotel carpet, which was so ground-in filthy he was afraid of infection.

Jeremy and Claire drove around the closed-up town, looking for an appropriately thin cat and talking about *the idea*.

"Here kitty kitty," Jeremy called out the window.

Claire figured to go all the way to Jackson Hole after they sold the first bathtub for gas money. "The richer the people are, the older they like their stuff and the more they'll pay for it," she said.

Jeremy could not disagree. He had once worked as a laborer on a rich people's house, and he'd seen the lengths to which those people had gone to acquire an old mantlepiece, door-knobs, recycled bricks, antique light fixtures, and a weathervane

NANCY LORD

pig that must have belonged to the Puritans, it was so worn-down by wind and rain. Claw-footed bathtubs, long and deep, were very much in demand by those same kind of people.

It would not be theft, not according to the man in the bar. The sanatorium had been abandoned for a long time. Already most of the valuables had been taken from it: copper wire stripped, doors unhinged. Half the homes in town, the man had laughed, had some of the old wooden chairs and dressers. What remained were most of the porcelain sinks, toilets, and tubs. Yes, the old-fashioned kind, the big claw-footed ones. Sick people had taken lots of baths.

Half a block ahead, a long gray cat slinked across the road. Jeremy ran the truck to the curb and got out with the milk. He swished the carton around over his head and sang a kitty-food jingle he'd picked up from his last stint of daytime TV watching. The cat reappeared from behind bushes, meowing loudly.

Only then did he realize he had nothing to pour the milk into.

"We need a bowl or something," he said to Claire.

Claire, curled into her corner of the cab, was snoring.

The cat, not fat, rubbed against Jeremy's boots and cried plaintively. Leaves on the trees overhead rustled, and wind chimes, somewhere, from one of the houses lined up behind fenced yards, made a tinkling sound that seemed to Jeremy even more pleading than the cat. How was it that people slept in those houses and then got up and went to work and came home and watered their lawns and cooked lamb chops for dinner and were more or less happy with all that? He, Jeremy, could not imagine living like that. Perhaps it was because, as his mother had always said, he was overly sensitive. He *felt* everything so much more than everyone else. If he lived in that house there, the one with the lighted porch, he would have to feed the cats and save the lambs and let the grass grow, and he would not sleep. Sad music—even the worst kind of country music—made him cry, and wind chimes were sad in the same way, especially now, at this minute, when he thought he must be the only person attentive to the world.

Jeremy sat on the curb and poured soured milk into the cup of his palm, and the cat lapped from his hand with a rasping tongue that was the physical equivalent of his own growing despair. In the light from the approaching dawn, the thin scar on his overturned wrist stood out, as hard as stone, as white as soap.

His friend—ex-friend now—Doug had said, "Of course you're depressed. Who wouldn't be depressed if they lived like you?"

But how did a person decide to live another way? And why? Jeremy looked at the house porch, with its hanging basket of some kind of flowing-over red flowers, its mail slot, an American flag flapping. He would be more depressed if he lived like that.

Doug had said, "Next time, don't call me."

Jeremy poured more milk into his hand. The cat drank. The sky lightened. Claire lay with her hair wrapped across her face and her mouth open. She snored without twitching. Claire didn't twitch because she didn't dream, ever. She was lucky like that. When she was awake she was completely awake, completely in the here-and-now, and when she was not, she was unconscious.

A low *who*-ing came from somewhere in the trees. Jeremy craned his neck but could see only branches, leaves, pieces of pale sky. Jeremy had always liked owls, liked the way they could turn their heads all the way around, liked their enormous eyes. He liked that they were around at night, keeping a vigil. They were quiet animals. They didn't get hysterical.

What he didn't like about owls was that they swooped down upon innocent mice, rabbits, even people's unsuspecting cats. Later, they coughed up those disgusting little packages of fur and bones. He had found these when he was a boy. He had pulled them apart to look at the bones inside, thinking he could reassemble them into tiny skeletons.

He would be God if he could make the perfect animal, something he imagined to be very much like an owl, only with a different appetite. A fruit-eating owl perhaps, or maybe one that fed on certain kinds of insects. (Jeremy had no great fondness for mosquitoes and biting flies, though he realized this caused an inconsistency in his reverence-for-living-things cosmology. He was still working this out.) His perfect animal would, like an owl, be feathered and quiet, solitary, and it would be most alive at night. Intelligent, of course, but in the animal way, instinctual, without thinking about every little thing.

Claire woke in a pissy mood and wanted Pop-Tarts, of which they had none. She was younger than Jeremy by two years and made on occasion these childish, petulant demands that Jeremy had learned to deflect with other enticements. In this case, he promised Domino's Pizza later, plus something for their thirst, but only after they had their tubs and gas money. For the moment, they breakfasted on corn nuts and sugar packets from the glove compartment. Then, still before any but the earliest of the town's risers was awake, they headed for the sanitorium.

It looked like an old, wrecked hotel, out in the middle of a field. Jeremy could tell it must once have been opulent, overflowing (as it still was) with porches and turrets and gables, and all sorts of interesting architectural bric-a-brac. It had been the kind of place where people sipped lemonades on the lawn while nurses in crisp whites tucked blankets around their legs. People used to go to such places when they needed a rest, to breathe fresh air and strengthen their lungs. This was the high-class way that people used to be treated for stress, and for depression, for what he thought they had called back then, simply, *melancholy*. Feeling overwhelmed? Life got you down? Take a month in the mountains. Take two. He felt an enormous sense of nostalgia, a great, pining neediness for the kind of understanding and care he would never find a way to, no matter how many of today's hospitals and rehab programs he checked into. Why couldn't he have lived at such a time? Why couldn't *he* be treated with croquet and hot baths?

"Cool," Claire said. She had brushed her hair and was feeling more generally enthusiastic, with the cat purring on her lap.

Jeremy parked the truck and they got out to inspect the building. It was posted, of course, warning trespassers to stay away. That was, Jeremy knew, just a legal trick so no one would be responsible if some kid got hurt playing in the ruin. There could be asbestos, too, and other kinds of bad stuff.

The main door was locked, but whole windows had been removed, frames and all, leaving the ground floor of the place as open as a honeycomb. Inside, peeling linoleum and warped floorboards were littered with broken glass and plaster. Wires dangled from a ceiling. Jeremy and Claire walked around to the back. There, the part that had been a kitchen opened to a sort of loading dock made of crumbling concrete.

"Wahoo!" Jeremy yelled, hopping up out of the grass and moving aside a sheet of plywood. Although the kitchen stove and sinks had been removed, the room they entered was still lined with long counters, and the wooden-shelved pantry beyond looked ready for restocking. Jeremy picked up a broken piece of crockery, part of a blue and white bowl or jug. He could imagine being served strawberries and cream, good country food. He loved this kind of place, loved the sense of elegance that remained in every last artifact. He wanted to run from room to room and claim it all for their kingdom, and he wanted to move slowly and let the experience unfold bit by satisfying bit, with a great clawed tub behind every door, or doorway, as the case might be.

Claire was already in the next room, crunching glass under her boots and looking into corners and alcoves, finding an old pair of underwear and, beyond, a grand and rickety stairway.

They went back to the truck for the two pipe fitter's wrenches that Jeremy, as though their present project had been destined, had come into possession of under somewhat mysterious circumstances just before they'd left their previous place of residence.

Upstairs, the rooms off the long hallway were small and cell-like, with—they hadn't noticed from below—ornately curved bars across the windows. "What kind of a place did you say this was?" Claire asked. "I guess they didn't want anyone getting away."

It wasn't that, though, Jeremy knew. Claire had never thought, as he had, about the attractive finality of throwing oneself from a height. It would not have been a good advertisement for the place if they had guests raining down on the grounds from unsecured lodgings.

Some of the rooms still contained their metal bed frames, their sets of springs. Each two rooms shared a bath, and each bath, indeed, held an old-fashioned bathtub, most of them partially full of rubbish. With no little effort, Jeremy and Claire managed to detach the one closest to the stairs. Only when it was free of its pipes did they realize quite what the size and substantialness of their prize meant. Together, they couldn't pick it up or even slide it across the floor.

Claire blew out her breath. "How the heck did they ever get this thing in here?"

Jeremy was figuring some kind of wheeled trolley, and then, unless there was an elevator he hadn't seen, some other kind of mechanical lift. In those days, labor was cheap. He and Claire would have to be creative. They did, after all, have gravity on their side. A come-along, and then planks on the stairs. Or they could remove some window bars and lower the tubs that way; he remembered a movie where a grand piano had been dangled out a window. How much were these things worth, anyway? He measured the end of the tub with his arms, then went back to the bedroom to measure a window. "How are your iron sawing skills?" he called back to Claire.

Claire had found a closet with rubber hoses and boxes of the world's oldest sanitary napkins, made from voluminous layers of coarse cotton. She modeled one between her legs, over her jeans. "No wonder women didn't used to be able to do anything."

"I don't know," Jeremy said. "Maybe right now we just take a couple of sinks and whatever pipe we can get loose."

In the end, what they carried away was one stained basin they could use in their new cabin, several sections of pipe that might or might not be worth something to a junk dealer, and a quite-nice picture frame that Claire ripped the back off of in search of, between it and its European landscape, an original copy of the Declaration of Independence or its equivalent. "Hey, you never know," she said.

Outside again, the morning was well underway, heat sneaking over the land. Jeremy stood in the armpit-high grass behind the sanitorium and smelled the air, clean and cloverly fragrant. Grasshoppers were rubbing their legs together; snakes were slithering. Overhead, some big bird circled. It was not a hawk and it was not an eagle; it had a large head and a square tail, like one of the great owls. Jeremy turned with it, watching it circle one way, circle the other way, flap, cruise, dive low as if to look at something, lift higher again, veer off toward trees, circle back again. He was barely conscious of Claire's complaining. She was hungry, she was thirsty, she wanted to go somewhere where she could take a shower.

The owl—if that's what it was—circled directly over him. He was sure it was watching him, sizing him up. It was late for an owl to be out. Shouldn't it be roosting in a tree somewhere, with its belly full of the night's incautious mice? Was it still hungry, hunting with desperation, hunting perhaps to feed the naked nagging hatchlings back in its nest? Or was it flying for pure joy, enjoying the last stretch of wing and slip across the sky before folding up for its rest? Jeremy studied the bird, the way it tilted, the way it swooped and picked up speed and glided, and he had no idea how it would be possible to tell a flight of desperation from one of pure and simple joy.

The bird circled, and he circled with it, turning his head and his body, spinning in the tall grass. He threw his arms out wide and spun faster, and the sky turned into a dizzy blur of blue, the bird an appearing and reappearing speck, the line of treetops a green streak. Grass blades slashed at his hands, and his feet stumbled over tussocks and viney undergrowth, so that he pitched one way and the other, hot and hungry and half-drunk or halfway to drunk again, flying across the land that would be his if only he had lived in the age of indulgence. He spun his feet right out from under his mad dance and crashed onto his back against the warm rootedness of trampled, sweet-smelling grass, with his arms out, and his legs out, as though he were holding back the earth itself from taking to the sky.

The moment that he fell was the exact moment that Claire drove the truck, too fast, around the corner of the old sanitorium. Jeremy knew, as he heard the engine race and grass snap under the tires, that she would not see him and that before he could even get his hands beneath him to begin pushing himself up, the inevitable would, as the inevitable is bound to, arrive upon him.

The Man Who Swam with Beavers

H E WENT AS FAR AS his two rented tanks of gas took him, and then the outboard quit and the world was wonderfully quiet, just the very small hollow-sounding slap of water against the drifting metal skiff. Once a line of dark birds flew past, so low and fast and near he heard their delirious wingbeats like a whir of something celestial, not music but less organized, fiber and air, there and gone.

The man sat in the bottom of the boat and let himself rock with the sea, and he looked up at the sun circling the sky and felt it warm on the top of his bare, balding head. After a while he stood up and could see an edge of land in the distance. After a longer time he raised himself again and the shoreline was closer. He could just make out a bouldery coast, v-shaped brown gullies folded into the pleats of high bluffs, dark spruce running uninterrupted along the top. In every other direction there was only open ocean and sky, gray and ceramic blue.

The skiff began to seem wrong to him: too even in its design, the welds like clay fingerprints, a railing and seats, too much domestication, the ridiculous large motor. He took up an oar, paddled with it first on one side of the bow, then on the other. The boat turned in circles, drifted, and came at last to land on the rocky, far-away, springtime shore. The man did not lift the motor; its skeg bumped in the gravel and among the rocks.

He left the boat there, grinding against the shore, and he walked on the beach until the boat was out of sight and he could no longer hear anything that sounded the least bit unnatural. He came to a break in the bluff, a gorge filled with budding green-ery and a rattling creek that ran to the sea. The man stopped at the creek edge and sat on a smooth rock.

He did not think. He sat. For forty-five years he had done nothing but think and plan and account for, and he was tired. This city man, a little fat, soft in the gut, divorced (twice), with children who did not seem to care for him; this indoor, unath-letic man who had gotten constipated rather than go on sum-mer-camp overnights and who, with multiple academic degrees, had needed lessons from the boat-rental person on how to start an outboard; this man who had rarely spent a moment by himself except in his car (in which, to be sure, he was always accompanied by radio or tapes), in sleep, and one time when as a boy he'd run away from home and hidden in a neighbor's garage for a small part of one afternoon; this man sat on a rock, hunch-shouldered in layers of sporty new clothes, feet spread before him in high, calf-tight rubber boots. He looked at the wide, arcing, endless ocean. He breathed slowly—the sharp air, the hint of salt—and he listened to water—liquid and light running past on one side, the solider silty mass mak-ing a slow shore-lap in front. He did not think about what he was doing in the farthest and emptiest place he could find on a map, a continent away from what he had called home. He did not think about what he'd left, or what he was hoping to find. He lifted his head and looked at sky. He lowered it and looked at stones that were round and flat and circled with rings, at peb-bles that were gray and black and red and speckled, and at clear, clear water cutting through the beach sand, leaving a honed edge, washing golden grains to the sea. He looked at where the creek met the ocean and saw how the waters mixed, the lens of flawless liquid spreading over gray, the clouding around the edges, swirling, joining.

After a time he noticed something swimming in the water, not far out, parallel to the beach. It had a black nose and dark, marble eyes, a head covered with chestnut-colored fur. It swam effortlessly, like a snake slithering through grass, its motor mechanisms hidden below the gray surface. When it came to the creek, it turned its head landward and floated ashore on the next lump of swell.

The man looked at the dripping animal, a yard from his boot, but it did not seem to be concerned with him. Without pause, it began to walk directly up the center of the creek. In its emergent form, it was no longer a sleek and slithery sea animal but a creature stout and waddling, wet fur stuck to its sides in sun-filled slicks. It dragged behind it a thick, black paddle-tail.

Beavers do not live in the ocean. The man had this single thought, pure reason, absolute knowledge gleaned from a lifetime of schoolbooks, televised nature programs, and colored magazine photos. He had never seen an actual beaver, as far as he knew, but he knew the creature before him was one even as he knew that beavers did not live in salt water. Always, he'd had this keen sense of what was *not* possible. He closed his eyes and opened them, and he was angry with himself for not believing. What was worth believing, if not this beaver tail, beaver fur, entire beaver walking out of an ocean and away from him now, not looking back, climbing over a drift log at the top of the beach, going up the creek?

What was real? Not the life he'd had yesterday, last week, a year and twenty years ago. Had he sat at a desk in an air-conditioned office, picking up telephones, talking about something called insurance? He could no longer see himself there. He could not picture himself in a suit, or a car, or wearing a fluorescent vest in a vain attempt at jogging. He could not hear the sound of high heels on a tile floor or bracelets clacking on a woman's arm, and he could not see a face on the pillow beside him, or the pillow. What was real was the ocean and the sand, the rounded rock beneath him, the beaver walking away, leaving him. Or leading him.

He caught up to the beaver in the trembling willows above the beach. It had stopped at the first green leaves and was eating, plucking and stripping, nibbling down a thin branch like celery. The man watched its graceful hands fold around another branch. It ate from tip to tip with a tiny clicking noise. He became aware of how finely shaped the animal's head was, the brightness of its steady eye. Tufts of wet hair parted back from its face in a manner he could only think of as beguiling, and its whiskers quivered. But what he found most attractive was the fullness over the upper lip, an aspect of overbite that reminded him of some other face long in his past, beyond remembering—a face that might have belonged to a teddy bear, a boyhood puppy, some downy girl-child in a smocked dress. It was not the memory that was important but the feeling that came to him now, of absolute acceptance, comfort, something as strong as love.

The beaver took a final chew and began to walk again up the creek, knocking rocks loose to clatter back behind. It glided through a pool, scrambled up a falls that broke over the top of a rock, waddled through ripples. It kept to the most-watered portion of the creek, as though water were its sole element, the centerline by which it steered.

The man followed.

Through willows and leafing alders, around boulders and tree trunks that had slid down the steep, sandy banks on either side, the beaver followed the creek and the man followed the beaver. The water rushed down cascading steps, flowed evenly over shallows. It foamed white and parted around rocks. It roared, deafening, and it tinkled like crystal bells. At the top of the bluff it spilled over one last lip. In the forest beyond, it lay flat and shaded, slowly moving, quiet. The beaver, immersed to its nose, swam again. The man crashed through alders and bushes alongside, pricking himself on devil's club thorns, ducking jagged dead branches. Ancient evergreens, splintered with age and draped with skeins of hairy moss, towered overhead. A spruce hen, unnoticed by the man, perched in a lower branch and merely turned its ruffled head to follow his clumsy passing.

After a time the man became aware of the sound of more running water, a higher-pitched and faster flow. The trees opened up, there was more sky, more light, and then the man stood below a log and stick dam and looked out across a cobalt, satin-finished lake. On the far side, meadows led to more forest and then to snow-covered mountains that pierced billowy clouds. He took the scene in very quickly, felt it strike him in the heart; it was unimaginably beautiful, beyond anything he could have dreamed. In the next instant, he missed the beaver. He climbed to the top of the dam, surprised at how solid it was, and he could see the beaver's reddish round head and rump, heading down the center of the lake, away from him, leaving a v-shaped wake that widened all the way to shore. For several long moments the man stumbled back and forth along the top of the dam, but, short of diving into the water, there seemed no way to stay with the beaver. The brush on both sides of the lake was dense and overhanging, a near-impenetrable jungle. The beaver never looked back.

The man fought off the feeling of abandonment. Beaver or no beaver, he understood that he had arrived at a place of significance. He sat and then lay on top of the dam, spreading his weight over a thousand stick points. He waited. Water trickled with a soothing, clean sound. Offshore, among the early spears of lily pads, fish jumped, plocking in a rhythm the man at first associated with perking coffee and then came to recognize as something far more sublime. The sun stalled just where the trees scraped the sky, lighting one whole side of the lake with a warm yellow glow. From far off came a sudden report. The man recognized the sound, though he'd never, not in his life, heard the slap of a beaver's tail on water. He heard the slap with that part of his being—down at whatever cellular level recorded genetic history—that shot the impulse like echo back to raised hair and quickened heartbeat. He was warned.

Birds sang out from the woods, trills and melodies that crossed over each other, blended, repeated in what the man could only decipher as joyous exaltation. He let the water music and the birdsong wash around him, and he breathed the scent of spruce needles and softened pitch. After a while he sat up and studied the dam: the interweaving of uncountable logs and sticks, all of them tooth sharpened, bare of bark. This was real work, work that held a lake together, a lake that held a world. He looked back across the water. The sun had fallen below the trees, and the surface had darkened. The fish were no longer jumping.

The man had known there were places like this. You found them through the backs of wardrobes or mirrors, or over the walls of secret gardens. He knew the stories from childhood, but he'd not been adventurous enough, then, to want to look in those places, to follow the storybook children. He'd wanted limits; always, he'd been the child who colored within the lines. Though he remembered this now: a print on the wall of the room in which he stayed when he visited his grandmother, a glassy river running through a glen framed by rock walls and fabulous weeping trees, and ladies dancing—fat ladies in bare feet and flimsy gowns. As a boy, the thought had come and stood at the edge of his imagination, like something glimpsed with peripheral vision—the idea of entering the picture, another time, when the fat ladies had gone home, when the glen and the cliffs could have been his own—but he was never brave enough, in his grandmother's house, to try. And then he had gotten too old to imagine such a thing and had forgotten, until this moment, that other moment of invitation.

He lay down again on the dam. It was night, but darkness didn't come. He sought the dark behind closed eyelids and listened to the water as it seeped and dripped and trickled and flowed beneath him. He could feel its movement as though it were passing through his own body, finding its way into crannies of bone and through the loose spots around his heart. Water filled him to the brim. It spoke a language that began with *yes* and *do* and continued in liquid clear syllables an entire vocabulary of possibility.

After a time he became aware of other sounds—soft snorts of breath and a whisper like leaves being swept across water. When he sat up, the lake was patterned with the tracks of two approaching beavers, the nearer one with the butt end of a branch fastened in its teeth. They came to the dam, climbed up over one end of it, and went to work, the one fixing the branch into place, the other scooping mud and a mash of reedy grasses and pressing the mixture, with probing hands and an occasional push of nose, into chinks in the structure. Both beavers were larger and darker than the one he'd followed up the creek. The first one disappeared into the brush; seconds later, alders began to shake. The man heard the grate of incisors on wood and felt his own teeth ache. A third beaver floated down the still lake and shuffled around the dam, gnawing a green stick in half and then turning it in its hands, like a corncob, to strip it of bark. It watched the man as it did this, and he watched the stick turn. This beaver was small, like the one he'd followed up the creek, but had a longer face and an angular, masculine chin.

There were many things that the man could not do, but he forgot what they were. He took mud in his hands and let the sound of water tell him where it should go, and he gathered weeds and rocks to fit among the sticks. In the woods, he circled among trails flattened by beaver tails and witnessed the many rounded stumps and clipped branches, and he dragged back to the dam a fresh branch of alder and tried to fit it along one side. He watched what the beavers ate—not just green bark, but the reedy underwater grasses, and he ate them too and found them sap-sweet and good.

He rested on the top of the dam. One of the large beavers sat very close to him, turned so that its thick, gorgeous, wet-fur back was facing him. The blunt edge of its tail touched his thigh, and he saw the perfect design of it, the overlapping scales and the stiff dark single hairs that grew from between the scales. While the beaver nipped at alder twigs, the man leaned closer. He held his hand out and, ever so carefully, let his fingertips touch fur. The beaver shifted its haunches away and turned a cool eye.

For a moment, a split second only, the man thought he heard the familiar first ring of a fax machine, but then it was gone and he was again in perfect wilderness.

They worked through the night, all of them together, and the man did what he could. In the forest, he used his weight to wrestle down a cut tree that had caught in the branches of another, and the bounce of it against the earth filled him with immense pleasure. The beavers, though, stayed away, and he realized that the tree was too old, had been hung up too long and become too dry to be of use. He tried to understand what the three beavers were to each other and how they felt about him coming into their midst, but each one seemed to work privately within established routines. Sometimes, though, he felt them trading looks behind his back; when he turned and caught their eyes himself, he saw neither wariness nor aggression but only watchfulness.

One beaver left and swam back down the lake, and then another, and then the last, and the man was left alone on top of the dam. He listened to the water trickle through, and it sounded different to him now, less urgent. He knew where the leaks were and he could visualize the exact sticks, the perfect dabs of mud and weed, that would block or seal them, and how each change would alter the sound. He heard the water carry away a particle of chipped wood and a grain of dirt and felt the whole dam settle minutely. The man slept with running water, grinding his teeth.

The next day the large beaver that had not sat beside him returned with two smaller beavers, and they all worked together, the man doing what he could. He moved more adroitly around the dam and was quicker to recognize the suitability of materials and what needed to be done. He began to recognize patterns of birdsong and the creaks of specific trees, and he watched two white-collared loons dive as though they were following the tips of their bills through invisible rends in the lake's surface.

The beavers swam off in the middle of the day, and he could only stand in shin-deep water and watch them go, ruddering with their tails. He walked in the woods and looked at the bell-shaped pink flowers on the berry bushes, but he did not like to go too far from the sound of water. When he returned to the dam, he watched the far end of the lake for any ripple and listened for the slap of tails, but the lake was smooth and still. He looked into the water below his dam-perch and saw the tiny fish there, old leaves, soft green algae, shrimplike bugs. When he looked down the lake again, he thought he saw, amid trees, a traffic light change from green to yellow. His right foot pressed firmly against the dam, speeding up. But no, it was all green, only green, the sun casting meadow and trees in golden light.

He drank cold water, cupped into his hands, from the lake, and his mind filled with a desire for logs of a certain length and circumference, and then he saw those logs interwoven in layers, and that it was possible to build himself a floating structure that would both hold him above the lake and manuever across it. He went to work, selecting materials from on and around the dam, careful not to disassemble any essential underpinnings. When the beavers returned later, they seemed unconcerned, and when they were gone again, the man found they'd left a stack of new-cut branches, exactly what he needed.

In two days he built his raft, and then he poled and paddled it away from shore and was on the water, floating and dry. A breeze helped push him down the lake, past ghost-gray trunks of flooded trees, slick trails that led up banks and into underbrush, bare drifting sticks. He floated with his face extended over the water, gaze fixed on lily stems and soft bending reeds and, over deeper water, straight down through a sunlit haze of plankton into absolute black. Once, a trout rose from nowhere, flashing its rose-colored, sequined side as it turned, and the man was so stunned by the sight he cried out. Halfway down the lake he came to a beaver lodge, tight against the shore and overgrown with a crown of new alders, and he knew from the age of its sticks and its smell that it was an old house, abandoned. One of the smaller beavers appeared beside the raft, circled, dived with a quick, playful slap of tail, and came up facing him.

The meadow drew closer, pale with old yellow stalks bent over new growth, and the lake stretched off to one side. When he rounded the corner, the man saw another beaver lodge, larger and fresher, like a haystack at the watery corner of the meadow. He paddled to the house, as close as his raft would take him, and he looked at the moatlike canal that circled it, the deep clear place that led inside. Other beavers swam around him, and he saw one beside the house and then gone. He heard noises, the mewing of babies.

For a second his mind filled with a spectral line of cold metal and glass photographs—his children, as bald babies and as toddlers, schoolchildren, high school grads. But they had not mewed. They had screeched and thrown temper tantrums, had been sullen and played obnoxious loud music. It surprised him that instead of actual faces he could only see their images fixed in frames, but then he could only see the frames themselves and a bare wooden desk, and it was as though that distant life was escaping his imagination as much as any other possibilities once had.

This is how he came to live, then, on a pile of logs and sticks in a lake, with beavers. He traveled from end to end to work on the dam, but mostly he stayed near the beaver lodge. When he left his raft, he wandered the shoreline and along paths into the woods, and he learned where the tender branches grew and that it was safest to leave a tree incompletely gnawed for a later wind to blow down. He watched spring grow into summer, the forest thicken and erupt into flowers and then green berries. He saw where the loons nested with their one fuzzy chick and got to know the vocabulary of their cries.

He observed the beavers singly and together, and he came to understand that the large beavers were the parents of the others, except that the young one he'd followed the first day had come down the coast from another, overcrowded pond—was, in fact, an immigrant to the lake, the same as he. As with any first love, the man felt a particular and ineffable attachment to that beaver, but he understood that his place was with the parent beavers, that he had much to learn at (as he thought of it) their knees. Besides, his beaver-love had already paired with an older son recently turned out of the family home, and together they were building a new lodge in the lake's farthest corner. The man helped, in his worshipful, awkward way, by moving logs and clearing pathways.

Most of the time, though, the man stayed close to the one-year-olds and the fearless new kits. When they were tired of wrestling and playing tag, the young ones climbed onto the raft and preened, combing their glossy fur with the nails of their

NANCY LORD

hind feet. They walked over him without the least shyness.

The parents, too, glided around the raft and sometimes brought him a new branch to be worked into its structure. He watched what they did, and how and when, and eventually he began to hear not only their snorts and silences and the clicking of their teeth but also their language, as though it were coming to him in words he could comprehend. They told him things he would not otherwise have known, serious lessons about eagles stealing kits and stories about brother hare and cousin moose. Mostly he listened, but sometimes he tried to respond with stories of his own. He could not remember much, but he sang themes from television shows he'd seen as a boy, Mister Ed the talking horse and M-I-C-K-E-Y-M-O-U-S-E. He remembered Rocky and Bullwinkle but couldn't recall any of their adventures, and so he could only report that such characters existed in cartoons, a fact that was not noted with much interest by anyone, including himself.

He lived in the world he knew now, a world of water and sky and growing things, and if he dreamed, it was only of forests full of young trees, of softest fur and a certain full and whiskered beaver lip. Every now and then some aspect of his earlier life would break through, and for a second he'd think he'd heard the beep of an alarm clock or smelled a turkey roasting, or he'd spot, behind a tree, the square corners of a chest of drawers or a flapping page of newsprint. These were always sudden—a beat or a glimpse or a quick inhalation—and then gone, a single synapse misfired deep in the memory vault of his brain. Their passing left him, always, with a sweaty sense of relief, as though the shadow of an eagle had crossed him and he was once again safe.

A day came in midsummer when the water lilies were open wide and gleaming under the sun and the man, sitting on his raft with his bare legs dangling in the water, realized that the water was no longer cold. He shed his clothes and dove in, and the water washed cool and clean all over him, and he heard, for a long second, what seemed to be music, oboes and clarinets, joyous measures of Beethoven's *Ninth Symphony* that rose and then faded and left him not relieved but elated, with a feeling he could only think of as *connected*. He opened his eyes to green, underwater light, and to beavers—long and sleek and perfectly graceful in their tucks and turns, fur pressed flat to their sides, hands fisted tightly against their chests.

The man swam with beavers. Although he had never been a good swimmer and tended to splash and flail in the water and could not stay under for long, his life now unfolded dimensionally, as though before he'd been stuck on a single flat plane. Below the surface, he saw lily stems sway with his passing and looked up at the dark undersides of pads. He watched fish skit by with vibrating tails and witnessed the wealth of stored food-branches anchored by the beavers in bottom mud. He gasped for breath and dove repeatedly, and the beavers teased him, good-naturedly, charging and veering away, brushing his legs and his shoulders ever so gently.

He swam again the next day, and this time the mother beaver turned toward the house and he knew he should follow. He filled his lungs with air and dove down and under and up through a narrow passageway, into a hollowed chamber. He pulled himself from the water onto a ledge blanketed with dry leaves and wood chips, and he lay on his side with knees tucked to his chest. The chamber was clean and close and smelled of

NANCY LORD

warm wet fur, wood, and moldering earth. Soft light seeped through the crisscross of overhead branches, and beavers snuggled against his back. Never, never, until this moment, had the man felt such absolute bliss, such a sense of finally having made his way home.

From that day on, the man lived in the lodge, coming and going with the beavers. He continued to help with construction and repair, he peeled bark from branches, and he swam. He slept at the center of the beaver family, cushioned in a circle of shifting fur, and was lulled by beaver murmurs. He began to dream beaver dreams of perfect sticks and higher water, of touching his tongue to his own long, chisel-edged teeth. He almost never had those odd, old slips of perception to some other time and place, and when he did, he could make little sense of them. Once he thought he saw a glass punch bowl in water close to shore, and it took him an entire day to puzzle out the name for it and to recall the dim concepts of *flavored drinks in ice* and *party*, utterly foreign people in incomprehensible activity. Ice, though, was a thought that stayed with him; the idea of frozen water was something he could feel, like a chill in his bones.

In time, the lilies shed their ocher petals, the trees bent to a north wind, and the lake grew cold again. The man, finally, could not immerse himself in the water without a gasp of breath, and his shivering and need for burrowing deeper into the heap of beavers became more acute. The weather change troubled him, but he could not give up the interior life of the lodge for a return to an entirely outside existence. Then one day he emerged from the woods with an armload of green sticks, and the entire beaver family was busy on the roof of the lodge, cutting and adjusting. In no time at all they'd fashioned a door he could open from either side. To secure it against the entrance of wolves or bears, the man rigged a sort of latch system that required his dexterous, uniquely sapient abilities to hitch and release. With this door, he was freed from the water passage and could come and go as he liked, in comfort.

In this way they all learned to live with the man's limitations. For each allowance given him by the beavers, he tried in some other way to make up for his deficiencies. His greater size and strength proved a frequent asset, since he could both move heavy logs and topple trees. Together they developed a system in which the beavers gnawed trees to their creaking points and then moved out of the way while the man made the final felling push; as a result, the beavers avoided the danger of falling trees without needing to wait for a windstorm. The beavers and the man, every day, added to their underwater stores of food.

Ice came, crinkling around the edge of the lake in lacy layers and then spreading and hardening across the water. Snow came and lay on the ice and in the woods. All of them slept a great deal—restful, deep, slow-hearted sleep. Periodically, the beavers dragged a new selection of water-softened branches into the chamber, and they ate and then slept again. Sometimes the man went out his door to stand in awe before the drifts of undisturbed snow, the silence broken only by the cracking of lake ice and cold-hardened trees. He loved to listen to the shattering pops of birch-woods and spruce, woods he knew so well now, in their barks, their grains, the itching of his teeth. Nights, he walked the frozen, windblown lake, and stars illumined the world.

Spring followed winter with higher sun and longer days, and sap ran in the trees. The ice softened on the lake. Little by

232   NANCY LORD

little open water extended around the lodge, and the woods began to empty of snow. Smells returned, and the sounds of running water, and birds. The mother beaver grew fat with new kits; when she rested against the man, he could feel the rumble of many heartbeats.

One morning very early, the beavers and the man woke with a start, as if from the shake of an earthquake. Three bears of enormous size, fresh from their den and very hungry, were attacking the roof of the lodge. Logs creaked and branches splintered, the entire structure rocked. The man reached for his door to check that it was tightly latched, but the bears, grunting and tearing, were digging straight down from the top.

The beavers huddled together, close, bodies flattened to the floor, and the man could feel them tremble with terror. Their eyes in the gloom were bead-bright. A roof log snapped and was jerked aside, and a shower of wood flakes and dust fell onto their backs.

The man, huddled and dusted with the rest, wanted to be heroic. He was large, after all; he had man-sized abilities. A sharp stick, if he had one, he could stab at the bears, fend them off, chase them away. But there were no sharp sticks in the lodge, nothing except ticklish twigs left from a meal, and nothing he could pull loose. The bears ripped apart more roof, and he could see daylight and then glimpses of huge, bobbing, yellow heads. He smelled bear smell, fetid and stifling.

A hole ripped wider and a paw stuck through, a paw bigger than the man's face, with long, straight, amber-colored nails.

The beavers moved, one following another as smooth and continuous as running water, slipping soundlessly into the pool and out the passageway. From outside came the warning slap of the mother beaver's tail, and then others, every tail slapping water.

The bears were ripping at his door.

The man dove, into clear, free, ice-cold water. He felt the cold go through him and stop at his heart, and then he heard again the slapping of tails on water, and they sounded as if they were in his own chest, the pounding of his heart, again and again, exploding outward into light. He kicked his legs and felt himself shoot forward, rapturously sleek and powerful, the pleasure of webbed feet, the ruddering by great black tail. He was warm now, and he was safe, swimming away with beavers.

Remaking the World

"**B**E CAREFUL what you wish for," Fern warned. "You might get it." Michael looked at her dimly. He had just wished for "everything in the world," by which, Fern thought, he meant every toy, game, video, every battery-powered expensive piece of plastic he had ever coveted, which would fill quite a few shipping vans, even considering his limited imagination. Michael was one of those children who you could not take into a store or even for a car ride without his begging to be bought every toy on the shelf, every shiny electronic whirligig, a ticket to every amusement park, everything and anything edible, especially if it was made from one hundred percent sugar plus coloring. This was not behavior she would have encouraged in any child, but she found it especially unappealing in a fattish, sluggish boy of eight.

Fern felt truly bad that she so disliked a child. That the object of her disaffection was the only spawn of her only daughter made the situation that much more difficult. That she had invited the boy to spend the summer with her, while her daughter dealt with both a new husband who was proving to be, not surprisingly, not quite the find she'd imagined, and a difficult, bed-prescribed pregnancy, was, at the moment, a matter for deep regret.

Michael, though, was beginning to get the idea. She had said *no* to "the world's longest pizza," a wildlife "park" with caged and tortured animals, and a remote-control exploding asteroid. Now he looked at her from the passenger seat, pale and whimpery, as though he, too, were having regrets.

Wasn't this all backwards? Weren't grandparents the ones who were supposed to spoil the children, let them stay up all night, get dirty, break all the parental rules? Fern, in fact, wouldn't have minded letting Michael climb to the top of trees or go without socks, but those kinds of transgressions didn't seem to be things Michael wanted to do. Michael would never strain himself to reach even the lowest branch of a tree. He had to have clean socks every day and threw his wet ones into the trash. What Michael wanted was to set all the rules himself and, particularly, to spend all the money. "It's only twelve ninety-nine," he'd whined about the asteroid.

Fern told a joke: What did the selfish soprano sing? *Mi-mi-mi-mi.*

He had no clue.

She pushed back on her head the White Sox cap she'd traveled with for twenty years. (Not for her a new souvenir cap at every destination; where did today's kids get the idea that ten-dollar caps were a daily birthright, and what did they do with them all?) Her cap had accompanied her through Louisiana oil swamps, Manitoba bear country, nuclear testing sites, Cuba, and Panama; it had been up in a hot-air balloon, dipped into acid-rain lakes, even in and out of downtown Chicago. All her adult life Fern had been going places, looking and listening and writing down what she saw and heard. She was interested in everything and had been a darn-good journalist, committed to Truth with a capital T, to making the world a more educated and enlightened place. Still was, even if business majors with no sense of history, never mind imagination or daring, were in charge now. At seventy-three she'd finally stopped arguing with pip-squeak editors. She was officially "retired," which for her

NANCY LORD

meant putting new tires on her old Volvo. She could not abandon her habits. Her reporter's notebook was jammed beside her seat, filling up with details and observations.

Cowboys for Christ, she'd seen on a church placard that morning. By herself, she might have stopped. Now she was sorry she hadn't. She wanted to find a militia meeting, too. She wanted to look at guns and the people who loved them.

But this trip was not on assignment, and not primarily for her. She'd promised Michael, and his mother, that she would introduce Michael to the history and the national parks of the West. They would camp, they would search for dinosaur bones and arrowheads, they would look up plants and birds in her books. They would smell sage and sheep shit and learn the stars in dark skies. They would follow Lewis and Clark's trail over the continental divide.

"Be a person on whom nothing is lost," she said now to Michael, who was fidgeting with his collection of bottle caps. She waited for a response. Anything. At last he looked up over the dash. He had that slackness to his jaw that made him look slightly ape-like, and a face of all-American freckles she found somehow annoying. Which was completely unfair, she knew— nothing the kid had any control over, his inheritance from an otherwise absent father. It was just that anytime he thought anyone was looking at him, he put on that squinting face that seemed to shout, very self-consciously, *Aren't I just the cutest little all-American boy?* Fern guessed his mother had set him in front of so many cameras for so many years that the pose had laminated itself to his personality.

"Henry James said that," she said. "Do you know who Henry James was?"

"No," he said. Too firmly, she thought. Petulantly.

"He was a great writer and critic. That was his advice to writers—'Be a person on whom nothing is lost'—but I think it's good advice for anyone. If you pay attention to things, you'll learn one heck of a lot."

While they were still in California, she told Michael about underground aquifers, and that all those green lawns and swimming pools could only exist in a desert because people were draining thousands-year-old water that, when it was gone, would be gone for what was as good as forever. She drove him to the gates of the Nevada Nuclear Test Site, where they got out and read the warning signs, and she told him about the nuclear testing program and the downwinders who'd been sacrificed for "national security." In Utah they looked at the Great Salt Lake, its rising height and flooding one more example of the havoc wreaked by human-caused climatic change. "We are really fucking up the world," Fern told the boy, who, she thought, winced not at the devastation he was to inherit (and was wont to contribute to) but at her choice of verb.

They camped most nights, though this was not Michael's preference. He didn't, it turned out, like to sleep on the ground. Nor did he like rain, dark, grasshoppers, walking anywhere, being apart from other people, drinking plain water, or eating food they cooked themselves. These things he mostly described as *icky*. He did like having a campfire if he could turn marshmallows into flaming torches and otherwise burn things (paper, plastic, wet socks). Fern pointed out constellations. She went walking by herself and returned with flowers she looked up in her books, by herself. Michael sat in the car, even when it was stopped, although he had made clear he didn't like Fern's car because it lacked cup holders; his stepfather's car, on the other hand, was very cool because it had the best kind of cup holders. When they drove, Michael read billboards aloud, with a hopeful sound in his voice. *Lariat Motel, free cable, pool, only twelve miles. Taco Bell, only six miles. Teepee Village, factory outlet.*

They worked their way north, through Idaho and into Montana. They wove back and forth across the divide on narrow logging roads, while Fern wailed at the views and the natural beauty that still remained in their overrun, overexploited country. Michael muttered something that sounded awfully like, "Seen one tree, you seen them all" and listened to his Walkman. At Lewis and Clark campgrounds, Fern read aloud from the expedition journals, thrilled by the idea of discovery and the innocence of the time. "Imagine," she told Michael, "a girl only a few years older than you, with a tiny baby, leading those men across these mountains. It blows my mind." Michael buried his head in a paperback called *Goosebumps,* involving, from what Fern could decipher, a knife, a noose, and an errant eyeball.

Fern knew she was being very judgmental. She should not, she thought, have been so vehemently lecturous about the evils of sport utility vehicles, but she could not stand for her grandson to admire a product that was so incredibly wasteful and polluting; she had given him the whole history of the American auto industry's avoidance of gas-economy and pollution laws, its deceit and subterfuge and pandering, with a digression into the wasteful habits of American consumers and their refusal to accept the real costs of burning up so much low-priced gasoline. After that, Michael stopped talking to her about cars and car accessories.

Fern knew it was hard to be a modern, affluent child. Things had been so much simpler when she'd been young, when children had not, in fact, been at the center of the universe. Grown-ups had gone about their lives, doing grown-up things, and children existed in a sort of subworld or shadow, doing kid things along with the chores that were, of course, expected of them. Parents did not consult children about which car to buy, did not make them special meals, did not allow them to plan the family vacation and otherwise dictate the family's life. Rather than feeling repressed and ignored, Fern had flourished in her freedom. She and her siblings and friends had been unto themselves—playing, inventing, working out whatever needed working out. A rainstorm gave them a great simple joy; they built dams in the ditches and floated sticks for boats. They sewed their own little nets to catch minnows and butterflies. They put on plays they wrote themselves, and dressed for them in whatever they could swipe from a back closet or mending basket. They did not expect manufactured toys except, perhaps, at Christmas, and then they did not expect the whole store.

Oh, she had not been a perfect child. She had been headstrong. She had insisted on being president of the Busy Bee Club, and had not let Ella Sue join. She had thrown chicken eggs at boys. She had stayed out after dark and climbed a water tower. Once, at a fair, she had gone into a tent she was not supposed to go into and had seen part of a human body she was not supposed to see. Surely, she had sometimes been annoying. Her mother had told her to "act like a lady." Her father had said, "Sit down, goddammit." Her parents never worried about her self-esteem; they didn't know she was supposed to have any, and neither did she.

Of course, she had *had* a child, too, though Chloe's childhood was much less clear to her than her own. Chloe had been a late and unexpected gift. For a few years Fern had had to make some changes; she traveled less and worked the phones more. Her husband at the time—a Blakeish, depressive poet— had been little help, but she'd had a fabulous woman named Mrs. White, who would come in on a moment's notice and stay for days, doing all the feeding, bathing, and cooing that any baby or little girl could want. Not that she, Fern, had been a bad mother. In bursts of devotion, she'd spent many hours scrambling around on the floor with letter blocks and rubber dolls, she'd done the stroller thing through all the parks and playgrounds, and she'd read piles and piles of books about kittens and mittens and moons. She remembered, too, with small pangs of guilt, locking herself in her backhall office on deadlines and not answering the tap-taps, kicks, and plaintive calls for *Mommy.* She had, in fact, on occasion yelled, "Go away!"

But Chloe had not, she thought, been particularly scarred. She'd been, fortunately, a child with inner resources. She'd been content to play with her dolls for hours at a time, to cut up magazines with her round-pointed scissors, even—premonition of what was to come—to fold and refold her little clothes and to arrange shoes in neat closeted rows. She was not, as it turned out, an imaginative child, but she was certainly orderly.

As Michael was, in his way. Michael liked plans. He wanted to know, before a day started, exactly what it would entail and where it would end. He had not a spontaneous corpuscle in his body.

Neither did he have inner resources. He couldn't, for the life of him, seem to think of anything to do with or by himself. He needed, it seemed, something manufactured, produced for his use; he needed something to *consume*. He could not draw on plain paper, but he would trail a pencil through an insipid maze in his "activity book." He would not toss pebbles at a rock in a stream, but he would beg to stop at a run-down miniature golf course. Bat a rock with a stick? No, he had to have an official Whiffle-ball set. Climb an actual hill? Not when there was a theme park with a fake plaster one.

Nights, when Fern lay awake in her lonely tent—Michael had taken to sleeping in the car, having rearranged the back to make a little nest—she pondered the state of American civilization. Maybe Michael wasn't the problem. Maybe it was the culture, and he was merely its product. (There was that consumer-driven *word* again.) Michael had grown up, like every other child in the day-care age, in organized groups, where every sandbox moment was structured. *Now you will pack the cup with sand and turn it over. Now you will have your famous label juice drink and watch exactly thirty minutes of video about a purple dinosaur.* Television had spoiled them for anything other than passive entertainment. Was that too easy—blaming television? Why did Michael mourn missing his favorite shows but not his friends? Why did he not know how to *play?*

They visited Yellowstone with its faithful geysers and camera-ready tourists; they attended talks about buffalo, wolves, and fire. They found a cowboy museum, a pioneer quilt museum, and a petrified tree, and even rode a Ferris wheel and other, more gut-spinning "amusement" rides. They watched pronghorn run like the wind and wild turkeys roost in trees. Fern dragged a smashed deer off a road by one rigored leg while Michael covered his eyes and chanted *icky, icky, icky.* Driving east through Wyoming, Fern stressed how important buffalo had been in the original ecosystem, particularly to the economy and culture of the Plains Indians. "Imagine," she said. "Seventy million buffalo, and in a few years they were nearly exterminated. All to take away the lifeblood of the Indians. How's that for government policy?"

In a good humor, Fern agreed to follow signs to a buffalo ranch. Once at the gate and shaken down for admittance fees, they were, to Fern's horror, bussed with a bunch of old people to a herd of slovenly domestic animals and encouraged not only to feed them alfalfa cubes but also to kiss them on their big, rubbery noses. Michael was nervous around the animals and objected to their smell, but he turned bright as a bulb once they arrived at the restaurant/gift shop, where Fern contributed to the buffalo trade by buying burgers, jerky, and postcards. (She did not, however, buy hides, painted skulls, horns, teeth, or a video of Tiny, the ranch's largest and most famous bison, in which said star presumably munched grass and flicked his tail. These omissions greatly disappointed a certain boy.)

They skipped Mount Rushmore and its presidential heritage, but Fern could not bypass the mountain carved to look like Crazy Horse. She did not approve of transforming perfectly good, beautiful-in-themselves pieces of natural landscape into images of people—it was so appallingly arrogant, so blindly anthropocentric—but the concept of making commercial kitsch out of both a mountain and a Native American offended her doubly. She was interested in the controversy among the Sioux themselves—the group that aligned themselves with the "chief" who had given permission to the obsessed German carver, and the others, who considered the whole thing a sham and rip-off. As they approached the mountain, she tried to get Michael to use his brain.

"Michael, what do you think Crazy Horse would have thought about having his likeness carved onto a mountain that was a major landmark, maybe even a sacred site, to his people?"

"I dunno."

"What if I told you that Indians never named landmarks after themselves? They knew they were only short-timers on earth, and the mountains and rivers were ancient. They respected nature for what it was, not what they could do to it. Do you think old Crazy Horse would have wanted people to chip away a mountain to make him a memorial?"

"No."

Fern applauded quietly.

When they reached the mountain, it was as god-awful-offensive as she'd feared, and huge, and swarming with tourists. She and Michael swarmed right along with them, herded through the gift shops at the base of the mountain. She could see that Michael wanted it all—the T-shirts, caps, turkey-feather headdresses, war-paint kits, totem poles. *Totem poles?* He had learned to stop asking, though, and only dragged himself along, forlornly fondling the objects of his desires like little whipped Oliver Twist longing for another bowl of gruel.

"I've got one word for you," Fern whispered. "Arrowheads."

They camped along the Cheyenne River, and Fern captured the most gorgeous, shimmeringly iridescent dragonfly she'd ever seen. When she showed it to Michael, he folded up behind hunched shoulders as though he thought it might attack. She hunted up a likely spot to find arrowheads, and, sure enough, ten minutes later found one lying in plain sight on the bank. Delighted with herself, and hoping the tangible, sharp-edged object—imperfect as it was, with an irregular side and a broken tip—would ignite at least a covetousness, she ran to show Michael. He turned it over in his hand, examined it carefully, and then handed it back. "I've seen better ones."

Of course he'd seen better ones. They'd been through a dozen small-town museums, and every one of them was packed with the arrowhead collections of every dead rancher in its region.

"But *I* found this one! Right *there!* Don't you think it's completely cool to be at this river and think about some Indian, maybe hundreds of years ago, in the same place, making this arrowhead?" Fern was flashing to all those times as a child when she'd dreamed away whole afternoons riding sticks for horses and digging up "treasures." She would have died to have found an actual artifact. "Maybe," she suggested, "he was a boy your age and still learning how to do the flaking thing, and this one didn't turn out very well, so he tossed it up the bank. Or maybe it was in an animal that was butchered here, and the tip broke when it hit bone."

Michael remained stoically impassive, like a caricature of a chiseled wood Indian chief.

"Don't you think about that? About someone else living here, and now *we're* here, and here's the *thing* that maybe *no other person has held since that Indian?*" Her passion, she knew, was overcompensating. The less Michael reacted, the more she must.

He made his cute face, which, Fern was coming to learn, was a nervous mannerism. "Not really," he said.

She couldn't leave it alone. "Well, what *do* you think about, sitting here by this river?"

"Honestly?" he said. "I was wondering when we could stay at a motel again, and could it be one with a pool. I've noticed that check-in time is usually three o'clock."

⁓

Michael, two or three swimming pools later, actually expressed an interest in seeing the Grand Canyon. Fern interpreted this as a positive sign, although she suspected that the word *grand* and the fact that the place was so famously popular were key.

When they arrived after a long, sweaty drive, Michael looked out over the rim with all the other squalling tourists, and then turned to look at a stuffed Garfield cat clinging by suctioned feet to the back window of a neighboring car. He did not want to walk even partway down the trail. It was too hot. It was boring. He wanted to go to the store and buy sunglasses to replace the ones that had burned in a campfire. He would go if he had new sunglasses and they could ride on mules.

"What's so great about mules?"

"Mules are cool."

"Why are they cool?"

"You can ride on them."

Fern wanted to extend his logic. Feet were cool. You could walk on them. Or run. Or hop. But of course that was not the same. Feet were too much work. And they didn't cost anything. The value of anything was, she was learning, in direct proportion to its monetary price.

NANCY LORD

Sure enough, he had to ask: "How much does it cost to rent mules?"

"We're not renting mules. They jostle you to death and fall over cliffs."

"I'll find out." He went, stiff as a little businessman, into the building with the giant gift shop. He would want to buy postcards. He would not look at the view for more than two seconds, but he would want postcards of it. He had, she thought, about fifty cents in his pocket, the change he'd asked to keep from their last snack stop.

Fern wondered if it was all right to let an eight-year-old wander around a tourist attraction on his own. Did strangers still steal children, or was it only parents that did that anymore? *Hey kid, let me give you a ride in my Bronco. And here's some candy, too.* She decided Michael would be perfectly fine having a little info-gathering adventure on his own, and getting away from stingy old Grandma for a while. As she was not sorry to have a breather from him, too. She settled herself at the rim and tried to imagine coming upon the canyon a couple centuries sooner, what a fabulous sight it must have been in its raw, unpeopled, pre-cliché splendor. Even now, when she blocked out the voices and barking, the slamming doors, the smell of overheated cars and greasy food—it really was a wonder. Heck, even *with* the crowds. The splendor didn't change just because someone spilled potato chips in the foreground and all those fat people were clicking cameras that would make the opposite wall look a million miles away.

He returned with the information that mule rides were only eighty-two dollars per person.

"No," she said.

"Yes," he said. "Let me borrow the money. I'll pay you back. I'll get the money from my mother."

This was new, this mom's pocketbook strategy. Fern could not understand why a mule ride was suddenly such a big thing. "Michael," she said, "you don't even *like* animals."

"Please," he said. "I'll pay you back."

"If you want to ride, we'll go somewhere where there's horses. A real trail ride, not clomp-clomp. That'll be much more fun."

"No it won't. This is more fun." He looked like he was about to cry.

Fern could hear Sylvia Rimm, the syndicated child psychologist, whispering to her inner ear about overempowered children and the adults who bargain with them. She did not want to fall into the bargaining trap, and she certainly was not going to give in to demands. Especially when she had no idea why stupid mules were suddenly such a big attraction and Michael, seemingly, could not say. "Seen enough?" she said. "Let's get away from this parking lot and find a place to eat our sandwiches and cool off."

He started to cry then, like a toddler having a temper tantrum. He swung his fat, muscleless arms and kicked her car in a tire. People turned to look.

"Get in the car," she said. She got in and started the motor. She put it in gear. "In the car," she said through the open window. "Or I'll leave you here."

He got in.

Now, she thought, she would drive to the nearest post office, buy their biggest box, stuff him in, and mail him to Chloe. c.o.d.

"I hate you," he said, face averted. "I wish I'd never come on this trip. I hate you and your stupid car. All you want to do is look at stupid things. You hate everything. You hate people using too much water and carving mountains and making nuclear dust and killing all the buffalo. You don't want people to do anything."

She looked at the back of his all-American head. By god, he *had* been paying attention after all. "I don't hate everything," she said. "I like looking for arrowheads and at the stars at night and turning over logs to see what lives under them."

"Like I said, stupid."

After that, neither one of them said anything. Fern drove with both hands on the wheel and tried not to feel stung. They were a pair, she guessed, hating things and thinking each other's favorites stupid. But she would still argue that her aesthetic was the responsible one, that America's buy-now, save-nothing, hate-nature attitude was delivering major trouble. It seemed pretty obvious to her, if not to a child, that if the air, the water, and the resources were destroyed, there wasn't going to be much future for anyone. If she were the Supreme Being, she would seriously think about pulling the plug.

Once, reading up on American Indians, she'd come across a Sioux version of the Great Flood that had so impressed her with both its biblical parallels and its warnings that she still thought about it. The account started by saying that the Sioux believed there'd been a world before this one, but that the people had behaved badly. The creating power—not God exactly, but close enough—caused a flood that drowned everybody and everything except himself, who floated on his pipe bag, and Crow, who flew above it all. When everything was flooded, the creating power took a turtle out of his bag and sent it to dive for a bit of mud, which he used to make land. He shaped new people out of clay and told them to behave properly. The Sioux—at least the old ones, she didn't know about today's—remembered that ultimatum: Dammit, people, do it right or I'll keep remaking the world until someone does.

After a while she said to the still-sniffling child, "I always thought I could change the world. I could make it better if I just told the truth."

⁓

They stayed in a motel that night, which was not capitulating because Fern had already made the plan and shared it with Michael. But the next day Fern parked beside the kind of stone-washed creek she liked, in red rock country, and she sat at a picnic table and read the journals of Lewis and Clark. She knew she was being sullen, a perfect match for her sullen companion. The situation reminded her in a discomforting way of the last days of at least two of her marriages, when she had gone about in a hardened way, ignoring the other, who also went about in his hardened way, until the wall of indifference between them was so solid there was no breaching it. She read her book while the boy pounded on his computer game and then wandered off into a grove of trees.

She was among the Nez Perce with Lewis when she noticed Michael approaching with a paper cup in hand. He came steadily, slowly, across the grass, peering into the cup as though there was some great mystery to its bottom.

"What have you got there?" she asked.

He didn't answer but kept coming toward her, finally handing her the cup. In the bottom lay a large brown and yellow caterpillar.

"My god!" she exclaimed. "What a gorgeous creature! Look at those spines!" The caterpillar's back was covered with thornlike, bulb-headed appendages of various lengths and thicknesses, all curling in different directions, like burned-out trees in a drunken forest. She looked again at the expressionless, waiting child before her. "But you don't *like* bugs."

"You do," he said.

Without any thought at all, Fern reached out and ruffled the all-American hair on her grandson's head. Then, setting the cup on the table, she put both arms around the boy and gave him one big, squeezing hug.

"No one," she said, "has ever offered me such a lovely caterpillar. Michael, you are a dear." She loosed her hold on him just enough to take a look at his face, and what she saw was the brightest beaming she'd seen in weeks. It could be, she thought with a jolt, that all this time he'd only been trying to establish his own value, and the only value he'd ever learned was measured by how much money adults would spend on him.

Later, flaming marshmallow asteroids around a campfire, Fern told Michael the Sioux story about the creating power remaking the world, and Michael told her his own made-up story about the evil monster and the good monster and the war for the world's largest diamond. It was a stupid, childish story, but Fern only smiled and asked a few questions about the weaponry of the two monsters and the number of their bloodshot eyes. She was not, at that moment, ready to remake the world, except in the only way that was humanly possible: one thought and one action at a time, by the only person she could herself change, even at her advanced age.

COLOPHON

The Man Who Swam with Beavers was designed on a Macintosh G4 computer in the historic warehouse district of downtown Minneapolis.

It was set in Caslon and Koch-Antiqua. Designed in the early 1700s, Caslon had fallen into disfavor in England until George Bernard Shaw insisted that the typeface be used on all his books. Then once again, it became the most popular face in England. This version was designed by Carol Twombly for Adobe.